D1167420

Too Many Secrets and Too Many Lies II:
Never Gonna Let You Go

By

Sonya Sparks

RJ Publications, LLC

Newark, New Jersey

The characters and events in this book are fictitious. Any resemblance to actual persons, living or dead is purely coincidental.

RJ Publications
Sunya_sparks@yahoo.com
www.rjpublications.com
Copyright © 2009 by Sonya Sparks
All Rights Reserved
ISBN 0-9817773-6-8
978-0981777368

Printed in the Canada

September 2009

1 2 3 4 5 6 7 8 9 10

DEDICATION

I would like to dedicate this book to my mom & dad.

In loving memory of GrandMira, Grandma Winnie and my sister Elaine

ACKNOWLEDGEMENTS

First and foremost I would like to give GOD all the Praise and all the Glory and to say Thanks for blessing me with creativity, making this book possible.

Thanks to my family for all of their loving support and encouragement. A very warm thanks to my wonderful husband Jeff, my two beautiful daughters Sennamon and Kierstin, my three handsome Michael, Christopher and Tyree. My brothers Bryan, Roy, Vernon, Tony and Alton Jr., and my sister Carlotta. My beautiful lil lady Akeemie.

My oldest and dearest friend Vonda Parker, I love you. Charmaine My girl, My sister I Love You.

I didn't forget about you Mack and Byron. And to everyone who's ever shown me love and support.

I would like to say Thank You to RJ Publications - You are extremely appreciated may GOD bless you and everything you touch.

And a very special thank you to YOU from the bottom of my heart for reading my book.

Chapter One

"Oh it's you. What do you want?" Kayla asked DeShun hatefully as she tried to close the door.

"Damn, baby, I'm sorry about the other day; I know how sensitive you are about your kids," DeShun said eyeing her red robe. He knew he should have gone home but his need to see Kayla had taken over.

Kayla frowned pushing the door up a little more. "Are you drunk or what?"

DeShun laughed, "Naw, baby, I just wanted to talk to you. Tymera told me last night yo nig-, I mean your *friend* was coming out today. I just wanted to apologize for how I acted."

"Ok fine; apology accepted. I gotta go." Kayla tried to close the door but DeShun pushed his way in.

"Damn, a nigga can't win with you, can he? I come over here and try to say I'm sorry and all you do is try to slam the door in my face. What kind of shit is that?"

"Look, I'm running late as it is; I got to get ready for work," Kayla told him.

DeShun laughed, "I bet if I had been your nigga you wouldn't be rushing to get to work, now would you?"

Kayla tied her robe tighter. "What do you want?"

DeShun smiled and touched her cheek softly then became angry when she pushed him away. "Oh, it's like that now?"

"Damn, DeShun, it's been like that for over ten years now. What's wrong with you?" Kayla asked him angrily.

"Damn, baby, you always were beautiful, especially when you're angry. And red is definitely your color," DeShun said looking hungrily at Kayla.

"Get out, NOW!" Kayla snapped at DeShun.

DeShun laughed then reached over and kissed her. Kayla pushed him away and slapped him. DeShun was stunned at first, thinking to himself, *I know this bitch didn't slap me*! He knocked the hell out of Kayla, making her fall to the floor exposing her firm, well-shaped legs and her most private area. Kayla pulled her robed together quickly and tried to run, but DeShun grabbed her by her hair, yanking her swiftly back against him. "Damn, you still look good. Let's see what I've been missing and yo nigga been getting," DeShun whispered harshly in her ear.

Kayla started swinging her fists wildly. She landed some very good punches on DeShun. He became so enraged he took his fist and hit her in the head, making her fall once again to the floor. When she shook her head, he knew she was disoriented. She managed to hit and kick him a few more times, but he only laughed angrily as he lost complete control. DeShun began ripping her delicate robe from her body. He had become so livid that when Kayla scratched him across his face, he hit her viciously and unzipped his pants then penetrated her ruthlessly, pounding away at her body until he came. Shocked reality set in for DeShun at what he had just done. "Kayla, baby, I'm so sorry." DeShun stood watching Kayla as she curled her legs up and cried. He felt horrible as he stumbled away from her house. He was still very drunk and very high.

DeShun still couldn't believe how everything went down that morning. *Damn, I can't believe I did that shit*, he said to himself. He had no choice but to admit that all of his partying had finally caught up with him. DeShun could not believe how he had lost control.

DeShun sat and thought about that incident. He shook his head as he thought to himself, *One thing I know for sure is that I don't plan on going to anybody's jail and I damn sho won't end up being somebody's bitch. Hell no, not the kid. Luckily for me, one of my bitches found this place for me to lay low until everything has a chance to die down. I never should have gone there and I damn sure shouldn't have kissed her, but she looked so inviting wearing that little red robe I simply couldn't help myself.* DeShun rubbed his forehead in frustration as he said to himself, *I didn't mean to hurt her but she shouldn't have slapped me. I honestly didn't mean to beat her ass that bad. I had been so high and I had just left one of Mo's parties, I couldn't sleep and Kayla was on my mind. Shit, I hadn't even realized what I'd done until it was all over. All I know is something inside of me just snapped.*

DeShun was irritated to know Kayla now completely belonged to someone else. It was difficult but he was forced into the realization that Kayla didn't want him and it was completely over between them. He would never admit it to anyone, but it bothered him, because deep down a part of him wished she was still his. Even though he got tired of her nagging and always wanting to talk when they had been together, she had been his girl and he'd loved her in his own way. The problem was that his cheating on her all the time came too naturally and he hadn't even the slightest desire to quit.

From the time of the rape, DeShun's conscience had definitely started working overtime. He was feeling guilty for betraying her for all those years and not being a real father to D'Neko and Tymera. He realized he had been wrong and even worst was the way he treated her when all she ever wanted was to just be with him. Regrettably, now she was going to be another man's wife and worse yet, his own son despised him.

The idea of Kayla being engaged to Damian was getting to DeShun, although he knew it shouldn't because he'd had more than his share of women. Seeing her today at the mall kind of did something to him; it made him think back to the time she'd caught him with another woman right before they had broken up. DeShun didn't even remember who the woman was, but they had been in a lingerie store buying the woman some things and it didn't seem to bother Kayla one bit when she ran up on them. That was the first time he knew he had lost her. *Shit*, DeShun thought to himself, *I had never bought her ass anything nice like that.* DeShun knew he only had himself to blame because over the years he allowed himself to get used to Kayla giving him all of her undivided attention and now that someone else was getting it, it bothered him. DeShun didn't know why but he could never stand the idea of anyone else being with Kayla.

Damn. DeShun wondered who was beating on his door this late at night. His heart started pounding so hard he could hardly breathe. Instantly he dropped on all fours and quickly crawled to peep out the nearest window. He didn't see a car so he swiftly moved to the other window across the room. He felt stupid being down on the floor when he realized who it was. He hastily stood to shake off his bad nerves and was just glad nobody had been witness to his crawling around like an idiot.

"What's up?" DeShun's cousin, Mo, said laughing as he walked in handing DeShun a twelve pack of beer. Mo's brother, Jarrod, followed carrying a bottle of brandy and a couple of plastic cups. Jarrod went straight to the kitchen brought back ice then poured himself a stiff one.

"What's up?" DeShun couldn't help smiling. He knew he would soon forget about Kayla because these two always brought a party no matter where they went.

"Aw, my man, you ain't gon' believe who I saw tonight." Mo popped a can and sprawled across DeShun's sofa then propped his feet up on his coffee table.

DeShun kicked Mo's feet off as usual then opened a cold one, he smiled and waited because he knew from

Jarrod's expression, Mo was about to tell him about some fine honey.

"I saw Kayla and her new man leaving The Black Knight," Mo laughed, as he hit Jarrod's leg.

DeShun smiled thinking of all the good times he had had at The Black Knight, which was locally-owned and the only good spot to hang out on a Friday or Saturday night.

"Damn, DeShun, I didn't realize that girl was still that fine. Why you hide all that? Hell, if she had been my girl, I wouldn't have been hanging out drinking all of the time and I damn sho wouldn'ta cheated the way you did." Mo looked serious for a brief moment as he and Jarrod shook their heads obviously not understanding DeShun at all, then just as quickly they started laughing.

"Yeah, I heard they're getting married." DeShun took a swallow of beer trying to sound as casual as possible.

"Damn, his family ain't nothin' but money. Kayla's hit it big-time for real." Jarrod continued laughing as he stood to pull out a blunt. "I'm stepping out back for a minute."

"Save some for me," Mo called after Jarrod. "DeShun, you ought to come outside and hit it. I know you don't smoke but it'll make you feel better; I know you got to feel bad, I would, 'cause we both know Kayla was a damn good girl and was crazy over your cheating ass at that. Now she's kicking it with a rich man. You've definitely lost out," Mo laughed.

Damn, DeShun said to himself, *I wished I'd never opened the door. I feel worse than I did before.* DeShun sat watching Jarrod slowly exhale smoke, he seemed so peaceful. DeShun killed the rest of his beer then poured himself a drink. He drank half in one big swallow then refilled his cup. DeShun knew Mo was thinking about the rape and all but he was too good of a friend to bring it up. DeShun had told everyone Kayla lied about the rape but he knew Mo knew different. DeShun stood to turn on the stereo then walked outside to join Jarrod. DeShun took a hit from Jarrod's home-grown herbs. DeShun needed to forget about Kayla in a bad way.

"Now that's what I'm talking about." Mo quickly jumped up then came out to put his arm across DeShun's shoulders. "How 'bout we buy more beer and liquor and call up a few freaks?" Mo eagerly suggested.

DeShun laughed to himself, *What the hell, I might as well continue to enjoy myself, bet Kayla ain't thinking about my black ass unless she's hoping it's somewhere behind bars.* "Sure," DeShun told him.

***

The next morning, DeShun felt awful and to top it off, some strange woman had her leg draped across his. He gently brushed her hair aside to better see her face. He groggily stood and hit the shower as reality sunk in at what occurred the night before. *Yazmeen,* DeShun smiled to himself because she was a true freak. *Damn, I need to slow down with the women.*

After getting out of the shower, DeShun was glad to see Yazmeen was up. She brushed against him as she made her way to the bathroom. DeShun's manhood became hard as he once again thought of the night before, but he still wanted her to leave.

The doorbell rang and DeShun swore under his breath after opening the door. He knew he was still drunk otherwise he wouldn't have opened the door without checking to see who it was first. *Damn, this is not what I need.*

Angela Bryson, one of the women DeShun was currently sleeping with, walked in as usual and sat down on his couch. Yazmeen chose that moment to emerge from the bedroom. DeShun took a deep breath because it was obvious she had stayed the night. DeShun swore again under his breath. *Damn, I hope these two crazy bitches don't start breaking my shit.* He leaned back just in case they decided to go at it. His head was throbbing painfully so he was not in the mood nor did he have any plans to break up any fights.

To DeShun's surprise Angela was very calm when Yazmeen emerged from his bedroom. He was shocked by Angela's lady-like demeanor. Angela's face was emotionless but her eyes held her true feelings. Yazmeen only acted as if Angela did not exist. DeShun wanted to laugh but he knew now wasn't the time. Yazmeen caught him by complete surprise when she leaned over and boldly stuck her tongue down his throat.   His manhood immediately came to life once again. He couldn't help staring at Yazmeen's voluptuous booty as she strolled across the room to leave. *Now if only Angela would follow suit,* DeShun mused to himself.

"Haven't *you* been busy?" Angela crossed her legs slowly.

It was obvious she was pissed but he didn't say a word, he just sat on the arm of the chair across from her and waited on what she would say next. "You do realize you can't continue messing around the way you do, it's not healthy for either of us. I only pray you're smart enough to wear a rubber," She said calmly.

Damn, she had to go there, DeShun thought bitterly to himself.

Angela adjusted her blouse then added, and DeShun swore in all his wildest dreams he never expected her to utter the words she spoke next, "Especially with our baby coming."

DeShun sat unmoving for a full minute before gathering his thoughts. He laughed cruelly because he knew for a fact he wasn't the only man she was messing around with, but he was having unprotected sex with her which put him as a very strong possibility. "So I'm supposed to be the father?" He asked in pure disbelief.

Angela seemed not to breathe for a minute as she eyed him hatefully. The way she looked almost made him a little uneasy and definitely sent an odd shiver down his spine. She stood slowly and said in a peculiar tone, "DeShun, I have to go now. But before I forget, I've already told Kayla about our baby. You really should stay away from her," Angela added before she turned to leave, "And don't go denying anything because I've been following your ass."

DeShun immediately became pissed and grabbed her arm roughly, "What the fuck you mean I should stay away from her? What the hell did you say to Kayla?"

Angela raised an eyebrow and smirked. She even had the nerve to speak to him as if he was dense. "Just some girl talk."

Guilt seized DeShun as he thought of what he had done to Kayla. He had to force himself not to think about it. "When did you talk to Kayla?" He asked furiously squeezing her tighter.

Angela jerked her arm free and laughed. "Right after her man dropped her off this morning. We actually had a good chat about old times." Angela must have seen the anger in him because she hastily took a step back. "I should go. I'll be back later when you're feeling better. Remember what I said about Kayla," She warned him as she looked around, "And don't worry, your secret little hideout here is safe with me," She added carelessly before quickly leaving. For the second time an icy shiver ran down his spine.

At least now DeShun knew how she always found out about all of the women he'd messed with, "That crazy bitch has been following me, and out of all the women I've had she would be the one to get pregnant." He laughed at his own stupidity. "Shit." He angrily threw a half -empty beer bottle across the room.

Chapter Two

Angela was angry as she fussed to herself, "I can not believe DeShun and his cheating ass. I should have known never to trust that man. I've given up so much just to be with his lying ass that I will stop at nothing to have him – I pity any woman that gets in my way! I even stopped messing around with Drake and aborted a baby just to have DeShun, and to think I'd been with Drake on and off since I was fifteen, and his ass asked me to marry him and I said no. Shit, DeShun is definitely mine especially now that I am pregnant again. No Kayla or any of his other little whores had better get in my way."

Angela paced the floor as she continued her rampage. "It really pisses me off to think how that bitch had the nerve to talk down to me like I was crazy or something. Shit, Kayla probably enjoyed DeShun's roughness that morning anyway. Lying bitch! I know deep down she still wants him, but if she knew what I knew she'd keep her happy ass with that man of hers, before I pay somebody to put some shit on her ass she won't be able to get off. And I got something for DeShun next time he's with another bitch. Stupid motherfucker better watch his back especially since I've made up my mind to risk losing this figure just to have a damn baby. DeShun best recognize with the quickness; I ain't no damn joke."

Angela knew she needed to calm herself down so she took a few deep breaths as she thought of Yazmeen. Angela had been surprised to see her at DeShun's. Last she heard, Yazmeen had moved away and Angela hadn't realized she was back.

Angela thought to herself, *Yazmeen was never*

anything but a nasty ho. She had a baby in the ninth grade and would always fuck anything breathing. Although, I do have to give her credit for looking good after the life she's lead, but it's obvious Yazmeen forgot the number one rule: Never fuck with a man of mine. I guess she forgot I had to beat that ass in high school after she fucked Drake, so once again her ass needed to be taught a lesson. No better way to start than by being the mature adult I've become and befriend her.

Chapter Three

"Mitchell, what am I going to do? Damian is going to be furious with me," Carmen mumbled nervously as she paced back and forth.

"It's too late to be crying now. What the hell were you thinking having drinks with that man? Now Damian is the one that's going to suffer. You know very well he may never forgive you for this," Mitchell snapped then added quietly, "You know, I'm beginning to wonder if you didn't sleep with him too."

Carmen sat down. "Mitchell, please don't start."

Mitchell leaned back against the desk defeated as he reread the legal document for the umpteenth time. "This is not happening."

Carmen thought for a moment then asked quietly, "You really think he might never speak to me again?"

Samuel Blackheart smiled as he leaned casually in the doorway. "You're probably right, but why should you care? You've never really cared about anything or anyone but yourself. Look at how you did Jordan. But I must admit Jordan and Damian both have quite a reputation in the business world; too bad you don't have Jordan's Power of Attorney too. But on a positive note, the both of you should be extremely proud of your boys. This marina Damian built is absolutely amazing. If I were a gambling man, I wouldn't be scared to bet in no time at all Damian will have something else going on. Hell, he can even help Jordan run their family business. The two of them together would be something to see."

"What the hell are you doing here?" Mitchell roared.

Samuel looked around proudly. "Well this is my

property now and it's all perfectly legal, but please feel free to have your lawyer look over our agreement. But don't forget because by my calculations, you only have about four days remaining to remove all of your personal belongings before they become my property also." He smiled as he turned to leave. "Oh and by the way, to put your mind at ease, Carmen and I didn't sleep together that night. Unfortunately, it's been quite a while, too long to be exact, since she's been in my bed."

"You're a real son of a bitch," Mitchell said coolly, as he barely managed to control his anger.

"You know, that's exactly what my father told me when I took control of our family business." Samuel left just as quietly as he had come.

"Well, this is going to be a hell of a shocker for Damian to come home to," Mitchell said grimly.

***

As he pulled up to the marina, Damian wondered what was so important that his mom and Mitchell needed to talk to him. He hadn't wanted to leave Kayla and the kids behind, but from the tone of Mitchell's voice he knew something was up and figured it might be for the best. He had a bad feeling and it got worse as he got a closer look at the man tying down a boat who was obviously giving out orders to people he didn't recognize. As a matter of- act, he recognized no one. "What are you doing here? Where are mom and Mitchell?" Damian couldn't help frowning.

Samuel laughed, "Damian, it's been a while, good to see you, son."

"That doesn't answer my question. What is going here?" Damian demanded.

"I take it you haven't spoken with Carmen yet," he laughed, somewhat taken aback by Damian's unusual rudeness as he easily sensed the fury in him. "Well, your mother sold me the marina. You've made quite a profit, I might add."

"What do you mean my mother sold you my marina? That's not possible, I own everything completely; her name isn't on anything pertaining to this place." Damian knew he was closely on the verge of losing it.

"Damian, you forget she has your Power of Attorney," Samuel spoke evenly, "Besides, your father already had your lawyers look over all of the paper work to make sure everything was on the up-and-up. Now I suggest you be on your way because I have a lot of work to do. Just go and talk with your mother; she'll explain everything. Son, I am truly sorry because I really do like you. Just remember - it's nothing personal, only business," Samuel said calmly without any remorse.

Damian was furious but after Samuel called him 'son' it felt like a kick in the gut because Samuel was his father's half brother. Damian didn't say another word, he only walked away. By the time he got in the car he was so angry he could not think straight. He didn't even think he could have spoken a complete sentence if he tried. He took a few calming breaths as best he could before driving to his mom's house.

"Damian," Carmen said as she opened the door, somewhat surprised at the intensity of the stare he was giving her.

Damian could tell she had been dreading this moment as she silently stepped aside for him to enter.

Carmen led Damian to the kitchen. Mitchell was sitting drinking a cup of coffee. From Damian's stance, Mitchell could tell he already knew about the marina so he only nodded his head gravely as he handed Damian a stack of official-looking papers.

"Have a seat, Damian. Would you like some coffee?" Carmen asked nervously.

"No." Damian stared hard at Mitchell. "Did you

have anything to do with this?" He asked, but for some reason he doubted it. Mitchell had been patient and understanding of the anger and resentment he held against him. Somewhere along the way he had actually gotten over it and had come to terms with what Mitchell had done, even though he still had a lot of unresolved feelings toward him for leaving them.

"No, he did not," Carmen said as she sat down at the table and sipped her coffee.

Damian angrily looked over the papers. "Then explain this." He waved the dreaded document in the air. "I do not understand, because this is the exact same offer Samuel made me years ago. I even told you about his offer and you knew I had no interest whatsoever in selling."

"Please sit so I can explain," Carmen said. "After Mitchell and I heard you and Kayla were engaged, we wanted to celebrate you, Jordan, and the lives you have made for yourselves. Mitchell and I were to meet for drinks after he'd finished at the marina, but he called to let me know he was tied up with one of the receiving trucks. He told me to enjoy my evening and he'd see me at home." She stood to pour another cup of coffee with unsteady hands. "Samuel came into the bar after I'd had a few drinks and we began talking. He seemed to be excited about your engagement and all. We talked maybe an hour catching him up on everything, and then he told me he had to leave and asked if I was ok. I stumbled when I stood so he offered to give me a ride home. He told me he would need to stop by his office to grab some papers he needed to work on over the weekend. I didn't think anything of it at the time because he seemed to be genuinely happy that you had met someone and decided to marry. When we got to his office it was late so he asked me if I felt like walking in the building with him so I wouldn't be left in the car alone. I went up and sat while he got his papers together, we had a few more drinks. I vaguely remember signing the papers, but by that time I was pretty much out of it." Carmen looked genuinely ashamed as tears fell from her eyes. "Damian, I can't begin to tell you how sorry I am."

Damian had heard every word his mom said but he still couldn't believe this was happening. "Do you honestly have the nerve to sit there and tell me that I actually no longer have my marina because you decided to celebrate my upcoming marriage with a man of his scruples? What is your problem? Did you forget all of the things he's done? Especially how he manipulated and stole his own father's company right from under him?" He laughed incredulously as he stood to leave. "You know, I really can't figure you out. You don't think sometimes, and I actually think maybe you actually believe the world revolves around you because to this day, I have yet to understand some of the things you've done, especially to Jordan and even worse, how you could have slept with Mitchell's own brother. Look at you; even now as old as you are, you are still doing stupid, irresponsible, unforgiving things all over again. I wish you'd just grow up for once in your life."

Damian turned to leave then stopped adding unfalteringly, "You know I really don't blame Jordan one bit for not wanting to be around you too much. Maybe I should follow his lead and stay the hell away from you as much as I can. Maybe it's even a good thing Kayla and I postponed our moving here until after our wedding, because I really don't want to live anywhere near you right about now." This had been the first time Damian had ever spoken to his mom that way, usually he just ignored her and the things she did, but he felt completely betrayed and hurt. For the first time in Damian's life, he slammed his mother's door when he left.

Damian drove back to the marina and found Samuel working on the *Carmen*, which was the very first boat he'd ever purchased. Without uttering one word or giving a thought to the fact that Samuel was his uncle, Damian hit him so hard he fell overboard. Damian left him sputtering in the water as people looked on.

Chapter Four

Kayla couldn't believe Angela had the nerve to knock on her door and think she still wanted DeShun of all people. Kayla shook her head as she mumbled, *the fact remains that he dogged me out then brutally raped me. Anything that I may have felt for him was now dead, gone and buried. That woman was more than welcome to him and his lying ass.* Kayla knew Angela was going to get everything she had gone through and more; Angela would never have any peace where DeShun was concerned. Kayla felt her anger rising even further. *And to think DeShun, with his sorry, no-count ass, had the nerve to get her pregnant when he has never even taken care of the ones he already has.* Kayla only felt sorry for the baby Angela was carrying.

Kayla had felt so good after Damian dropped her off; even though she hadn't had much sleep she knew she was going to have a good day. *Well,* Kayla said to herself, *Angela just spoiled all of that with all her stupid shit and adolescent drama. I hope DeShun comes back over here just so I can have his ass locked up just for getting me caught up in his shit all over again. And that woman better be glad I didn't give her smart ass a straight beat-down for getting all up in my business.*

Kayla decided to sit on the porch until the school bus ran, but as she reached for the knob, she started shaking as fear suddenly consumed her. She jerked her hand away and took a few calming deep breaths, "Get a grip, girl. There's no one on the other side of that door," she said aloud, angry at herself for not being able to control these sudden attacks. After a few moments she finally got up enough nerve to open the door. Kayla sat quietly wondering where DeShun might be.

***

Kayla thought about how ever since the incident, D'Neko and Tymera felt like they had to protect their mother. Today after completing their homework, they all played basketball and ended up competing in video games. Kayla had to admit it was fun and knew all they really needed was to just relax and let everything go. They played for hours and after the kids went to bed, she poured herself a glass of wine and relaxed for the remainder of her evening. As she sat, she thought of D'Neko. She felt the tears well up in her eyes as she couldn't help but think all too clearly how he wasn't fooled by what his father had done to her.

Kayla forced herself not to think about the rape so she thought of Damian. Yesterday morning he had gotten a message to call Mitchell. She and Damian had been out so he had to drop her back off at the house before leaving. He wasn't due back for a few days because while he was there he wanted to check and make sure everything was ready for when they moved.

Kayla and the kids hadn't really been alone in their house since everything had happened and it was hard. She couldn't help imagining DeShun standing on the other side of the door every time the doorbell rang. No matter how hard she tried she couldn't shake the image of him assaulting her. Kayla wouldn't admit it to anyone but that was one of her main reasons for being so excited about their move. She had grown to hate her house because the fear of being there alone never went away. She did not feel safe and every day she stayed in her house, her panic attacks grew worse.

Kayla had just finished her wine and poured herself another glass when Damian surprised her with his sudden appearance. He kissed her on her forehead and sat down quietly beside her. Kayla smiled. "You're back early. What did you do, turn around as soon as you got there?" Something seemed to be off with him so she poured him a strong drink. "Here, you look as if you could use this."

Damian half smiled. "Thanks," he said as he continued to sit on the sofa deep in thought.

"Feel like talking or do you want to be alone?" She asked, sitting on the arm of the sofa and waiting on his reply. It was obvious that he was more than just tired; she could tell something was really bothering him.

Damian pulled Kayla down onto his lap. "There's been a change of plans; we're not going to be moving yet." he absently played with her hair as he took a big swallow of his drink. "The marina has been sold. My mom signed it away to my uncle."

Kayla saw the hurt in his eyes. She also saw the anger that lingered passionately there and wondered how his mother could have done such a thing. "Damian, did she have some type of reasonable explanation?" She asked gently as she caressed his face.

Damian kissed the palm of her hand. "No." He leaned his head back and closed his eyes. "I don't understand any of this. She of all people knew how hard and long I had to work to get the marina to where it is."

"I'm sorry." Kayla tried to get up.

Damian held her down and frowned as he looked at her closely, "Sorry for what? You're not the one that signed those papers; my mother did that all by herself."

"I know that, it's just if I had not opened the door without checking to see who it was first you wouldn't have felt compelled to stay here for so long because I never would have gotten…" Kayla tried to explain but Damian cut her off.

"No," he said firmly, "it wasn't your fault. You

didn't ask for what was done to you, and I stayed here because I wanted to be with you and the kids. None of this is your fault and I don't ever want you thinking otherwise."

Kayla laid her head on Damian's shoulder and relaxed. It felt good to her to have someone there for her for a change.

"Well, Miss Kayla, first thing in the morning we're going to get us an agent so that we can find us a bigger house." He pulled her chin up so their eyes were level. "Don't worry about me. Just focus on planning our wedding. Now," he said kissing her, "let's go upstairs and practice this husband-wife thing."

Chapter Five

After leaving the realtor's office the next morning, Damian dropped Kayla off at Jordan and Ashland's house then went to visit Jordan at work. Damian tried convincing Kayla to quit working for a while even though they were not moving, but she loved her job so she wasn't hearing it. "Besides," she told him, "I can hardly wait to surprise Ashland with the news of us not moving."

When Damian entered Jordan's office he casually replaced papers back inside a folder. "Damian, how's everything going? Are you all packed up yet?"

"We're not moving," Damian replied.

Jordan smiled. "Kayla finally convinced you to stay?"

"Actually, our mother made that decision for us," Damian said indifferently.

At the mention of their mom, Jordan sat back and studied Damian intently for a moment. "What happened?"

"She sold my marina to our beloved Uncle Samuel," Damian said cautiously trying to keep his anger at bay.

"Really?" Jordan was surprised, "How in the world did she manage that without your signature?"

Damian laughed. "My stupidity compelled me to give her my Power of Attorney years ago. I had actually forgotten about it."

Jordan thought quietly for a moment as he unconsciously tapped his pen against his desk. He had been shocked to learn that The Blackheart, which was what Samuel was better known as, was actually Mitchell's half brother. Jordan had known of Samuel but had never had any dealings with him personally. He also had never been impressed with any of his unsavory business practices. Jordan suddenly smiled broadly. "Well, maybe this is a sign." He walked around his desk to lean against it. "Why don't you come here? This company is just as much yours as it is mine." Jordan raised his hand to cut Damian off from whatever protest he was about to make. "Before you say 'no' just give it some thought. It's not the carefree life you're used to, but who knows, you might even like it. I'll personally show you the ropes; all you have to do is work with me everyday, attend meetings and I'll teach you everything I know. Hell, you may even end up being more hard-nosed than me." Jordan smiled then abruptly changed the subject. "Now lets go have some lunch, I'm starving, besides I'm meeting with Jermaine Sanders today." Jordan laughed, "I'm quite impressed with his resume even considering the fact he's Sierra's younger brother."

Damian laughed. "In other words, Ashland wants you to give him a chance."

Jordan laughed jokingly, "Very good, little brother, I do think you'll do quite well in this thing we men love to call shackles and chains."

***

"Jermaine, you're young, but I like the way you think. What do you say, Damian?" Jordan asked Damian.

Damian looked at Jermaine quietly for a moment. "I think he would definitely be an asset to the company."

"Well then it's settled. Welcome aboard. I will see you in two weeks." Jordan waved for their waitress. Jordan noticed Jermaine reaching for his wallet. "I got the check. You just get plenty of rest over these next weeks because once you start you're going to have a full workload."

Jermaine only smiled and stood to leave. "Oh, I almost forgot." Jermaine looked embarrassed. "Ashland called me last night and made me promise to bring these and give them to you." He handed Jordan an envelope, "They're pictures of Chelsea, Devlynn and Deacon."

Jordan laughed. "I'd almost forgotten myself that she did tell me you had something for her."

Jermaine laughed. "I have a lot of things to take care of so I guess it's time for me to get back on the road."

Damian watched Jermaine leave the restaurant. "He seems a lot older than he is."

"I know," Jordan frowned slightly, "Kind of reminds me of myself a little when I was his age."

Damian laughed. "That can't be good."

Jordan became serious. "Do you want your marina back?"

Damian frowned. "I showed you the contract mom signed. Mitchell and I even had it checked out. It's solid, all perfectly legal."

Jordan raised an eyebrow. "If you come aboard, I will personally see to it Blackheart signs your marina back over to you."

Damian laughed but noticed Jordan was not even smiling. "You're serious, aren't you?"

Jordan stood. "Yes, I am. He legally took it from you and I can just as legally take it back. Let's just think of this as a wedding gift. I'll get your marina back for you under the condition you come and work with me at our company for six months. Then if you decide to move back there, I won't bother you ever again about working with us. Besides, it would make grandfather happy. He's been meaning to discuss this with you anyway." Jordan smiled because he knew at the mention of their grandfather Damian would finally give his offer some serious consideration. Jordan dropped a large tip on the table. "Think on it, but right now I need to get back because I have a lot of work to do."

Damian stood slowly and thought *what the hell*. He needed something to occupy his time. "Alright, Jordan, I'll be in first thing in the morning. But I have one stipulation."

Jordan raised an eyebrow. "And what is that?"

"That I don't have to wear a suit and tie everyday," Damian told him seriously. He couldn't help it but ever since he was a small boy, their mom would make him wear one every Sunday and every Sunday he dreaded it.

Jordan stared at Damian for a moment then all of a sudden started laughing. "I can handle that. Dress pants and dress shirt and no tie, except during business meetings, then I expect to see you in a stylish business suit, little brother." Jordan held out his hand to seal the deal.

***

Kayla and Ashland were sitting in the flower garden.

"So we won't be moving to Virginia," Kayla said.

Ashland said shocked, "Wow, is Damian ok? I know how much he loves the marina."

"I can tell it's bothering him deep down but he's dealing with everything really well," Kayla laughed, "unlike that brother of his. I can only imagine how Jordan would have reacted if that had happened to him."

Ashland laughed.

Kayla stared intently at Ashland for a moment. Even though she was laughing and talking there was sadness about her. "So how are you and Tylen doing?"

"All of that is completely behind us now. At first I was furious but I did a lot of thinking and Jordan really helped me to see that what happened between my mother and Tylen occurred long before we were born. I love Tylen and I can see why my mother fell in love with him. We're good," Ashland said sincerely.

Kayla thought to herself, *you're better than me. I'm just glad Bianca is your mother and not mine.* "I'm glad to hear that."

Ashland thought sadly of her mother and of Marcus not really being her father as she stood to pick a flower. She wasn't quite ready to talk about it with Kayla yet. Marcus still didn't know so after she and Jordan discussed everything with Devin and Bianca they all agreed to keep it a secret until Bianca had a chance to tell Marcus.

"Ashland, is everything alright? You don't really seem yourself," Kayla asked frowning.

Ashland smiled and handed the flower to Kayla. "I'm fine. MeShayla just kept me up last night."

"I can not imagine going through that again," Kayla laughed as she smelled the flower, "Especially with Michael being only eleven months old."

Ashland laughed. "Careful now, Damian might want a little one, one of these days."

Kayla frowned only making Ashland laugh harder.

Ashland stood. "Come on, let's go get pampered."

At the salon Kayla and Ashland were having a good time. Kayla had called Damian to let him know where to pick her up. She and Ashland had just completed their body massages and were getting pedicures when Damian walked in.

Damian smiled as he looked down at his watch. "I'm early," he said as he kissed Kayla and took a seat beside her. The Korean lady who was working with Kayla looked up and asked him if he wanted a pedicure. He laughed shaking his head no.

A petite old employee got up from her station leaving a well dressed woman sitting as she walked away. A short time later a disturbance near the back caught everyone's attention in the salon. The owner was arguing heatedly with the petite old lady. Other employees laughed as they continued working. The owner thought no one could understand except the Korean workers. They continued to argue then a few minutes later the little lady angrily grabbed her things and left. The owner assured everyone that everything was alright.

Ashland and Kayla only looked at each other and frowned. The Korean lady doing Kayla's feet only snickered knowingly at Damian as he laughed out loud during the argument.

Kayla and Ashland looked at him curiously.

Damian laughed. "I'll tell you later."

The owner put on some gloves then sat at the station his employee had recently vacated then looked down at the woman's feet. He unintentionally made a dreadful sound. Other employees nearby tried not to laugh but was having a hard time containing it. The woman looked embarrassed as she put her shoes on and discreetly left.

Ashland and Kayla looked on curiously while admiring the very pretty woman dressed in designer clothing as she walked by. Damian was embarrassed for the lady as she quickly headed toward the exit.

As soon as Damian, Kayla and Ashland got outside Kayla grabbed Damian's arm. "Tell me what was so funny."

Damian looked around briefly. "The little Korean lady didn't want to do someone's feet."

"Whose feet?" Kayla asked curiously.

"The lady dressed in Chanel," Damian said.

Kayla smiled. "She had on some bad Blahniks."

"So, what had everyone laughing and what exactly did they say?" Ashland asked.

"The little lady said," Damian laughed, "she was not touching her feet because they looked as if mold was growing on those filthy old talons of hers. The owner told her to either do it or go home for the rest of the day. The little lady told him to do it then she quit, telling him to fix his own damn dinner when he got home." Damian laughed as he added, "The little lady was the owner's mother."

Ashland and Kayla laughed.

Chapter Six

Angela had gotten off early from work and to her surprise, she ran into DeShun while she was shopping at a mom-and-pop store. She was surprised when he asked her out to dinner then suggested they either go to a club or catch a movie in the next town over. That evening after she finished dressing and sat down to drink a glass of gin and juice, her doorbell rang. Angela smiled as she thought, *DeShun must have changed his mind and decided to pick me up after all.* Surprisingly she found Drake standing in her doorway looking as delicious as ever. *Nothing but the devil in disguise,* she reminded herself ruefully.

"What are you doing here?" Angela asked unsmiling. Drake smiled in that provocative way and she knew he would try something if she let him in. He seemed too sure of himself so she grabbed her keys and walked out locking the door securely behind her. "I was actually on my way out to get something from my car. We can walk and talk on my way there," she said forcefully, thinking he had a lot of nerve just showing up unannounced.

Drake laughed knowingly. "It's been a while and to be honest, I miss you. You're looking damn good these days." He put his hands in his pockets as they walked. "So tell me, what man has you looking so good tonight?" When they stopped walking he caressed her cheek gently as he leaned down and kissed her. His kiss was demanding and caught her completely by surprise. She pulled away as imagines of other women appeared in her mind.

Angela thought, *now go figure that one, he even sounded slightly jealous when he asked me that, out of all the years we had been together he never once showed an ounce of interest in how I looked or dressed.* Angela laughed nervously as she opened her car door and got her sweater out. "Drake," she began politely, "he, whoever he is, is none of your business. Now next time I would appreciate it if you would please try and call before showing up."

Drake laughed teasingly. "Ok I can do that, what's your number. Or did you forget you had it changed?"

"I'm sure you'll find a way to figure it out." Angela turned on her heels and left him standing there. He was actually smiling which really pissed her off because he was just too full of himself.

"Angela," he casually called out, "a few minutes just for old time's sake. Come on, you know you want to."

Angela thought for a moment then smiled. *What the hell.* "Ok Drake but don't get it twisted, we are still not together." She dialed DeShun from her cell to let him know she was running late.

As soon as they entered Angela's apartment she pushed Drake up against the door and unzipped his pants. She let out a shaky breath as she unleashed his throbbing, swollen member. Now she remembered why he had her ass so crazy. Drake held her head as she licked the head of his amazing power tool. She teasingly slid her tongue up and down his hard, powerful shaft before taking him fully into her mouth. Like the true veteran that she was, she licked and sucked every inch of him.

They eased onto the floor as her mouth work its toe-curling magic. She heard him moan loudly when she took each one of his love sacks fully into her mouth and started humming. When she ran her tongue slowly up the crack of his ass she felt him shudder. Once again she performed pure magic on his impressive, swollen manhood. He tasted so good that she took him further down her throat. Her pussy was now soaking and throbbing to the point she felt she might explode if she kept at the pace she was going. She had no choice but to mount him, letting her pulsating pussy squeeze him tight as she rode him in a steady gratifying rhythm. "Oh, Drake," she moaned as he teased and sucked her swollen nipples while squeezing her buttocks tight. Angela was in pure ecstasy.

After Drake left, Angela rushed to clean herself up and get ready for her date with DeShun. Yazmeen had called to chat about nothing in particular so Angela had to hurry her off the phone. *All Yazmeen ever talked about was men, shopping, partying or weed.* Angela mused, *her ass really get on my damn nerves sometimes cause what she really needed to be doing is taking care of that kid of hers.* All Yazmeen wanted to do in life was have a good time. Angela had learned this early on after befriending Yazmeen that night she had slept with DeShun. Angela laughed as she thought, *I couldn't really blame her because DeShun is so damn fine and all, but her ass still crossed the line where I'm concerned. Now she must pay.*

Chapter Seven

Jermaine was getting ready for dinner and thinking about how fast time had gone by. It had been almost two months since he started working with Jordan and Damian. He loved his job because he got to do a lot of traveling. On one of his business trips to Virginia he had meet a woman named Madison and shortly afterward they began seeing one another. Surprisingly Madison was Damian's ex but Jermaine liked her even after he learned this. He'd never forget the day he had first laid eyes on her. A woman he had been messing around with kept blowing up his cell phone so he had to get the number changed. He laughed as he thought about her trying to say she was pregnant and the child might be his, just to try and keep him. He had to set her straight, because ever since that incident with Bianca he always wore the raincoat.

Jermaine had been angry that day as he walked down the street and stopped when he saw Madison through the window deciding on which cell phone to buy. There was something about her that made him go inside that shop. He had instantly felt that pull of attraction when she asked him which one he liked best. After that day they began seeing one another.

There had never been another woman who had him thinking about her all the time except for Desiree Jones, a.k.a Bianca Kendrix. He poured himself a drink to help push Bianca from his mind. Women came too easy, especially when you had a little money, but Madison seemed to be different and he was definitely feeling her. But it still wasn't enough. No matter how mysterious or captivating she was there was still something missing. After

Jermaine learned Desiree's true identity he refused to allow himself to become emotionally attached to anyone ever again.

Jermaine admitted to enjoying his time with Madison. She was cool with him, especially because she didn't make subtle hints about when she would see him again and she wasn't possessive wanting him to spend all his free time with her which always instantly turned him off. Ultimately, she only wanted what he wanted -- good sex. He grabbed his keys to go pick her up and prayed she wasn't another Bianca.

Chapter Eight

Damian had almost missed the dinner party Jordan and Ashland were having at their house. Luckily his trip had been cancelled, but now after seeing all of the guests he wished he had stayed home with Kayla. "Kayla, we need to talk. I need to explain," Damian said quietly.

Kayla eyed him irritably, "Damian, now is not the time, we can't ruin dinner, Ashland went to a lot of trouble tonight." She handed him the green beans and left him standing in the kitchen.

"What's taking Damian so long? I hope he's not sneaking into the dessert already," Ashland said jokingly.

During dinner everything seemed to go ok and Damian was quite thankful for Megan's constant chatter because without it he wasn't quite sure how he would have made it. Madison worked for his 'Uncle Samuel' and was very close to him; that's how they had originally met. He really didn't know too much about her since she led a very private life, but Damian almost choked on his food when Madison started talking about her daughter, Mallory, which he never knew she had, but she quickly brought up Mallory's father. Then she spoke of her parents and what it had been like with her sister after their parents had been killed. He was surprised because he never knew she had a sister given she had never spoken of her, which struck him as odd since they had dated off and on for a while. This was until Samuel found out and made such a fuss about Damian dating one of his employees that they ended it. Then to top everything off, all of a sudden she started telling funny stories about their past. Jermaine was amused by it all, but Damian could have easily disappeared when he looked over at Kayla. After dinner Kayla laughed and talked with everyone for about an hour then politely excused herself.

"Kayla, it's been wonderful meeting you, we definitely have to get together again real soon," Madison said sweetly. Kayla only smiled and left.

Neither Kayla nor Damian spoke a word as they walked to her car. He opened her door and said, "I'll be home later. Jordan and I have a few things to go over."

"Whatever," Kayla said carelessly.

Damian only nodded his head in understanding and stepped back, he knew she was upset at him for not telling her about his relationship with Madison. Besides, he thought to himself, he didn't even know Madison would be here. He admitted he should have told her about her, especially with Jermaine dating her but with everything that had been going on he had honestly forgotten.

Kayla turned to get into her car then stopped. "You could have at least told me about her."

Damian stood dumbfounded as she got into her car and drove off.

Jordan and Tylen were in Jordan's study reading over some papers when Damian entered.

"Well that was nice; too bad Carmen and Mitchell weren't able to be here. I think they are having a better time than any of us right about now. So tell me, Damian, are you as impressed with Jermaine as Jordan and I? And Madison, she and Jermaine look nice together, don't you think?" Grandfather asked.

Damian was surprised Tylen mentioned Carmen because for some reason, he was angry with her. Lately they couldn't be in the room together five minutes before some sort of argument would erupt.

Jordan laid his papers on the desk and went to stand by the window.

Damian was pissed at himself, at Jordan for not

telling him Madison was going to be here and everything in general, so he took a deep breath before he responded, "I'm very impressed with Jermaine and yes, they do look nice together."

"She seems to be nice. She's a gorgeous little thing," Tylen teased as he glanced over at Jordan.

Jordan laughed and Damian sat back in his chair unsmiling. He was worried about Kayla. This had been their first disagreement and he wasn't quite sure how she was going to react when he got home. He definitely didn't feel like fussing and arguing but knowing Kayla he was in for a long night. Before he realized it, he turned on Jordan. "Next time you invite my old girlfriends over, respect me enough to let me know." Damian stood and poured himself a drink.

Tylen was smiling. "Well, Kayla's not happy, I take it." Tylen leaned back in his chair, "Pour me one while you're standing there." Grandfather gave Damian a stern look when he was about to protest to his drinking. "Damian, tell me something, why haven't you let Kayla know about Madison before now? I know you remember me telling you about what happened with Jordan." Tylen laughed glancing at Jordan as he took a swallow of his drink.

Jordan ignored his grandfather's remark and sat unsmiling in one of the chairs in front of his desk as he asked Damian seriously, "You ok?"

"Yeah," Damian took another shot of whiskey, "Kayla's just a little upset, but we'll work it out." He sat in the chair beside Jordan, "Enough about that; tell me how things are going with Samuel."

"Actually Jermaine has it almost taken care of so don't worry about it. You'll be in control again before you know it." Jordan stood to refresh his drink.

"Well it's about time for us to hit the road so if you two will excuse me, I'm going to find Megan and the kids, then we're going to be off. Be sure to remind Kayla we'll have D'Neko and Tymera back in three weeks." Grandfather said then stopped at the door as he suddenly began laughing. "Oh by the way, Ashland told me you spoke Korean. That's perfect because I have a Korean contact I want you to set up a meeting with. I'll call you with the details later." Tylen's laughter could still be heard even after he left.

Jordan laughed, "I can only imagine what her feet must have looked like."

"Trust me you don't even want to know," Damian said chuckling.

"Do you speak any other languages?"Jordan asked.

"Spanish and French, and I know enough German to get by," Damian said then added, "it really came in handy when I ran the marina."

Très Impressionné," Jordan laughed. "J'ai une réunion avec quelques contacts la semaine prochaine. J'aimerais pour vous nous joindre."

"J'aimerais à. Où ce sera-t-il?" Damian asked.

"Angélique vendredi à 6:00pm," Jordan said.

"Je porterai là le procès et le match nul très élégants," Damian said laughing.

Jordan laughed as he poured them both another drink.

Mrs. George stood in the doorway shaking her head sternly at their drinking and speaking in a language she didn't understand. "I hope you two are not planning anything illegal up around here." She turned away quickly when she heard MeShayla crying.

Jordan and Damian laughed.

Chapter Nine

It had been a few days since DeShun had seen Angela; he wasn't complaining because he realized that the woman was crazy and couldn't help but wish she wasn't pregnant. He'd invited her to dinner just to see where her head was and she was completely convinced they were going to be together. He had been feeling depressed since coming to the realization of how reckless and irresponsible he had become where sex was concerned. The past few days had given him a lot of time to think about things and he definitely didn't want to be a father again. He already had another child out there that no one knew about and he didn't need anymore. The idea of Angela being the mother to a child of his was more than he could take. DeShun laughed miserably, *the damn baby will more than likely be all screwed up and crazy by the time it's even five.*

Kayla was still on DeShun's mind and he knew that was the reason he was sitting in a parking lot close to where she lived, like a fool, contemplating his next move. This was his second time sitting in this parking lot debating whether or not he should face Kayla. He was too scared to make a move because he wasn't sure how she would react to seeing him again. He didn't know why but he needed to ask for her forgiveness. After about thirty minutes he finally got enough courage to go knock on her door.

"What's u-," DeShun began but Kayla instantly lost control and punched him in the face before he could finish speaking while simultaneously yelling at him, "are you stupid or what? How can you stand there after what you did to me and have the audacity to say what's up?" Kayla shook her head in pure disbelief as she punched him again. "You stupid-ass motherfucker!" She didn't think about pulling out any earrings she just continued punching him forcefully. Kayla had so much pent up frustration and anger inside that she fought him like a man. Kayla punched him once again in his face. DeShun was trying to maintain control as he tried blocking her punches but he was loosing it fast. Kayla kneed him in the groin, he doubled over then she instantly punched him in the face. As he was falling down he grabbed hold of a chair with one hand to try and stabilized himself and pushed Kayla off him with the other arm. Kayla stumbled over a chair.

DeShun stood frowning as he wiped blood away from the corner of his mouth. "Damn, Kayla, I only wanted to come over here and apologize. I didn't mean for all this to happen!" DeShun said angrily as he tried to help her up.

Kayla looked hatefully at his outstretched hand.

"Kayla, I'm sorry for hurting you," DeShun said and thought how what he had done was probably completely unforgivable. His anger subsided.

Kayla had stopped crying but her eyes were still full of tears and anger as she continued to stare at him.

For a moment DeShun couldn't think of anything to say because Kayla was so angry and silent. The torment inside grew with the intense look of hurt and hatred in her eyes, a look he knew he was responsible for. He briefly thought of how badly he had abused her, the remembrance was so unsettling now that he was sober and coherent that he shuddered. "For what it's worth, I truly regret everything I did to you. I know deep down you'll never be able to forgive me. I know I screwed up bad and crossed the line and all I have to say is I never stopped loving you."

You stupid motherfucker, all you can say is you never stopped loving me, Kayla thought vehemently as she continued to stare furiously at him.

DeShun was unnerved by her stare and wondered if

she would attack him again. He began talking about the first thing that came to mind. "I'm also sorry Angela came over here with all her craziness. I hope she didn't get too out of hand." He laughed as he thought of something his cousin, Mo, had said about pregnant women and hormones. Angela is bound to be off the hook in a few months and he knew he had to try and get her out of his life one way or another.

Kayla said heatedly as she stood, "Look, it's all good so why don't you just go home because I really don't want to get in the middle of you and Angela. And let's just leave everything else in the past." Kayla frowned, "Tell me, have you ever stopped to realized that maybe, just maybe, I had a few problems of my own? Or are you still so self-absorbed that you can think of no one but yourself? Besides, what you do or don't do with Angela or anyone else is really none of my business anymore; I know you haven't forgotten we are no longer together, which means I am no longer a part of your life. So stay the fuck away from me and leave me the hell alone."

DeShun looked hard at Kayla and asked, "You ok?"

Kayla felt herself becoming angry again, "You're pathetic."

"Kayla, I just wanted to apologize." Before Kayla could walk away DeShun grabbed her and hugged her tight, more so for himself than to show her affection. He instantly felt her body shake and tense up. The next thing he knew Kayla furiously kicked him then started swinging her fists. He grabbed her quickly pulling her close then held her tight, "Hey! Hey! I'm sorry. I won't hurt you ever again. Kayla, please be still and calm down." DeShun repeated desperately, "Kayla calm down." DeShun took a shaky frustrated breath then whispered in her ear, "I love you. I swear I won't ever hurt you again."

Kayla was crying and he felt he was on the verge of tears himself. Without thinking he kissed Kayla. Kayla instantly jerked away then slammed the door in his face.

DeShun rubbed his leg as he thought of Kayla. He knew she was right; he never thought about anyone's feelings but his own. He thought of his children. Tymera would always love him but he wondered if D'Neko could ever love him again. DeShun limped quickly to his car just in case Kayla called the police.

Chapter Ten

Angela was beyond angry and the jealously she felt made everything seem worse. She thought to herself, *here I am following that stupid motherfucker and look where we ended up. I knew her ass still wanted him.* Angela patted her purse because she knew she was going to have to start bringing out a one from her collection of hard metals. *I'll deal with DeShun later but as soon as DeShun leaves, me and the little ex are going to come to a definite understanding of things, once and for all.*

Angela made her way up Kayla's front door when it suddenly opened. She caught Kayla off guard and rushed by her, pushing her way into her house.

"What's up, Miss Thang? Are you having trouble on deciding which man you want? You know that man of yours is awfully sexy and we both know DeShun ain't shit, so why are you allowing him to come back into your life?" Angela knew she somehow had to calm herself down. She took a deep breath and waited on Kayla's reply.

"If you know he ain't shit why you want him?" Kayla asked.

Angela stood completely still and laughed as she eyed Kayla hatefully. Staring at Kayla made her jealously heighten even more.

"Look, Angela, for the last time, I don't want DeShun," Kayla stepped closer to Angela with a raised eyebrow, "but if I did, I could have him just at the snap of my finger and he would come running back."

Angela couldn't control it any longer, something just snapped and she ended up grabbing Kayla by her neck and putting the cold metal of her gun next to Kayla's temple and said forcefully, "Now let me tell you one last time and just maybe your ass won't be stupid this time. Leave DeShun the fuck alone or I'm gonna fuck you up so bad they won't be able to recognize you, and for good measure, I'll split your body down the middle with my shiny new machete sending our precious DeShun one half and that fine-ass boyfriend of yours the other. Do I make myself clear? I'm warning you, Kayla, don't make me have to come here again."

Angela knew she had the upper hand because she was the one with the gun but she had to let Kayla's neck go because Kayla looked at her in such a way it startled her. There was something indescribable glistening in Kayla's eyes but fear was no where to be found. As soon as Angela let her go they went at it.

"Bitch, how you gone come up in my house and pull a fucking gun on me over some piece-of–shit-of-a-man?" Kayla was outraged.

Angela barely got away as she quickly retrieved her gun and left. She was a little shaken because Kayla managed to pull a small patch of weave along with her hair from her head. Angela had been so angry when she saw DeShun kiss Kayla that she needed a good fight but surprisingly, Kayla was more ghetto than she actually appeared. *Shit, the bitch is crazy*, Angela thought and left just as quickly as she came. Inside her car she fixed her hair and makeup as best she could, because it was now time for her to pay DeShun a visit.

"Hey, baby," Angela said sweetly as DeShun opened the door, "can I use your bathroom?" She ran off in the direction of the master bath, before he could answer, so she could double-check her appearance.

When Angela returned DeShun was sitting on the sofa flipping through the channels. She knew better than to bring up the fact that he just left Kayla's, so she did the next best thing: she sat down beside him then swiftly unzipped his pants and deep-throated him so good that his struggles to push her away ceased completely. Right before he was about to cum she eased one of her hunting knives from her purse because she knew when it was over he would push her away. When he came, she licked and swallowed everything completely. Before he could gather his wits she grabbed his now deflated prize and joy and lightly began to run her knife over his chest and stomach, circling his manhood every so often just so he'd know if chosen she could easily take it completely away from him.

"Angela, what the hell is you doing? What the fuck is wrong with you?" DeShun said boldly for someone at such a disadvantage.

Angela laughed wickedly, "DeShun, DeShun, DeShun, when are you ever going to learn to take me serious? Not even three days ago, I requested that you stay away from Kayla and here you go not granting just one simple request. DeShun, what part of my request was it that you did not fully understand?"

"Damn, baby, if I'd known you'd be this upset, I would have never gone over there." He smiled that smile that always weakened her so she decided to let up on him a little.

"Ok, baby, I forgive you this time but let's not do it again." Angela put away her knife but held her purse close. "I'm really sorry. I shouldn't have pulled that out like that but I sometimes get crazy jealous. As long as I know you love me and our baby, everything will be ok." She kissed DeShun then stood to leave because she knew she'd gotten her point across. "Hey," she said sweetly before she walked out the door, "are you going to swing by so we can have lunch together tomorrow?"

"Yeah," DeShun said sounding strange and breathless.

Angela got in her car pleased. *DeShun ought to know better; I ain't a damn fool. I'd never hurt the one thing that gives me such overwhelming pleasure.* Angela wanted to laugh, but she had to pee so bad she knew she would pee in her clothes if she did. Her cell rang and it was Yazmeen again wanting her to smoke some weed with her. Angela laughed in disbelief, *Sometimes I believe her ass is on some stronger shit. I am too sick of her and it is time I handled my business.* Angela decided to make one stop before heading to Yazmeen's house.

"Hey, girl, what's up?" Angela asked as Yazmeen opened the door. It was too quiet inside which kind of made Angela uneasy so she hesitated before entering.

Yazmeen laughed at her, "Girl, come in and be quiet; Lil Man just fell asleep."

Now Angela was royally pissed and if she had any second thoughts about what she was about to do, they quickly left. *How her stupid ass gon' call me to her house to smoke some damn weed while her child is asleep in the other room?! Stupid bitch!* Angela smiled as she made herself comfortable on one of the floor pillows.

Yazmeen brought Angela a bag of weed and told her to roll them a few joints while she fixed them some Crown. Angela did as she was told then they smoked a joint. Yazmeen left the room for a minute, so Angela quickly pulled out a little baggie of her own whitish mixture and stirred it into Yazmeen's drink.

Angela held up her glass. "A toast to new friendships."

"I got one better: here's to men, men and more men," Yazmeen laughed pathetically as they clicked their glasses.

Angela finished off her drink and poured another. Yazmeen's phone rang and Angela heard her invite some men over.

"Girl, we got two hard, hot bodies coming over as we speak," Yazmeen said.

"I can't. I have an early day tomorrow," Angela told her.

"Well I guess I'll just have to take care of them myself," Yazmeen laughed ridiculously as she finished off her drink.

To think, her son is in the next room. I've had enough of Yazmeen. Angela stood to leave and hummed to herself as she casually walked the few blocks to her car. The baggie had been a mixture of pure opium, PCP and crushed valium pills.

Chapter Eleven

After leaving Jordan's house, all Kayla wanted was to be left alone. She was more jealous than she had actually realized or wanted to admit. She really didn't feel like being bothered with anyone and DeShun was the last person she expected to see. And Angela was the last person she wanted to think about or deal with. She really didn't need any of this today of all days. And she especially didn't need to hear DeShun tell her how he still loved her after all these years. There was a time when she'd fool herself into thinking DeShun would do right, but their kids were eventually scarred by everything no matter how hard she had tried to protect them. *No, DeShun is no longer a factor in my life,* Kayla reminded herself.

After Angela left, the reality of what happened set in. Kayla sat with her arms folded around her legs drinking a glass of straight vodka. It had taken forever to get her limbs to function well enough to fix her drink. When she regained control of her nerves, she was so angry she couldn't think. "Crazy-ass bitch! Her and DeShun deserve each other," Kayla mumbled and was shaking as she picked up the phone to call Ashland. "Can I meet you somewhere?"

Kayla could just imagine Ashland frowning when Ashland hesitated before asking if she was ok.

"I'm fine. I just really need to talk to someone right now," Kayla said.

"Meet me at Misty's," Ashland said. Kayla hung up the phone then grabbed her purse to leave.

Chapter Twelve

Damian was about to turn down his street when he noticed Kayla and a man on their front porch. Kayla was actually in the arms of another man. *Now isn't this some shit! Maybe I wasn't the only one keeping things,* Damian thought irritably. Damian's guilt over not telling Kayla about Madison was getting the best of him and to top everything off, Kayla had just let another man kiss her, no matter how brief it was. Damian instantly couldn't do anything but keep driving straight before his anger took over. He needed time to cool off.

Shortly afterwards Damian made his way back home. Kayla was gone so he sat back on the couch drinking straight whiskey. Everything seemed to just fall apart in such a short span of time. He hadn't realized his cell phone had been ringing and whoever it was didn't leave a message. Just as well, he thought, because he did not want to talk to anyone. When he realized it had been Kayla he was actually glad he missed the call because right now as angry as he was with her he didn't think it was a good idea to talk her. Even though he wanted to find out who the man was and whether or not she was still with him. The man had seemed very familiar and after a while it finally dawned on him who he was. Damian became even more incensed.

Chapter Thirteen

DeShun sat on the sofa after Angela left, too shaken to move. He thought about her asking him to take her to lunch and became angry. "Why did I ever fuck with someone I work with and especially that crazy bitch?" De Shun rubbed his head in frustration. "Shit, I wish I could quit my damn job, but I got to pay this motherfucker to stay here." He yelled angrily, "Fuck!" He knocked everything off the coffee table onto the floor and yelled, "Why can't her ass get fired on some of that stupid shit she be doing at work."

DeShun needed a drink in a bad way so he stood and found nothing stronger than a beer. His doorbell rang and he ignored it, the next thing he knew Mo was walking in with a bottle of Remy.

"What's up, cuz?" Mo said handing him the bottle then retrieved two glasses and ice from the kitchen. "Thought I'd bring a little something 'cause when I tell you what I got to tell you, you're going to need it."

DeShun happily sat down and filled his glass, drank it all then refilled his glass again, "What's up?" He asked but from Mo's look he knew it wasn't going to be good at all.

After taking off his hat and taking a long swig Mo said "You need to watch your back. I was talking to Angela's sister last night and she told me some things that worried the shit out of me."

To hear that Mo was worried of something perked DeShun's interest and had him a little unnerved; he was already beginning to tremble a little all over again.

"Yo, last night we were sittin' around chillin' and

she got a little drunk and said some crazy things about Angela." Mo stirred his drink.

DeShun only laughed because Angela *was* crazy, but he did wonder why Mo was hanging out with her sister.

"You know she said Angela is into collecting weapons. Their old man collected them and Angela was always fascinated, so her dad had left all that stuff to her when he died."

A cold chill swept over DeShun as he remembered Angela moving that knife so expertly over him.

After taking a long swallow, Mo continued talking. "She heard Angela down in their basement the other night making a big commotion about you and Kayla. She at first thought Angela had company but after a while she realized Angela was fussing out loud by her herself. And your girl, Kayla, is number one on her shit list, which is definitely not good at all."

DeShun continued drinking as he listened to Mo.

"Remember Marsha that lived over in the Crossing, you know, the one that disappeared when we were in high school?"

DeShun frowned as he shook his head wondering why Mo was bringing her up after all these years. Marsha simply vanished one day after school. He thought of all the months of searching that everyone had done and she was still never found. He quickly downed another drink, because all of a sudden he didn't think he wanted to hear the rest.

"Well, she told me the day Marsha disappeared, she had seen Angela earlier that morning take one of the hunting knives from her father's collection cabinet. She hadn't thought too much of it at the time because Angela was always moving stuff to piss off their father when he wouldn't let her go somewhere. But later that night her father was fussing with their mother about touching his things. It had caused a huge argument and their mother told him she hadn't touched anything and stormed off, but the next night it strangely reappeared in the cabinet, all polished and shiny. She said she wouldn't have thought anything of it except, number one, Angela hates to clean and number two, Marsha and Angela had a bad fight the day before over Drake. She can't really prove anything but Angela had been on a rampage fussing and acting ill towards everyone around the house, but the night Marsha disappeared she was unusually happy." Mo leaned up and said in a low tone of voice, "She thinks Angela had something to do with it." Mo killed the rest of his drink then poured another, then added very seriously, "You need to leave that crazy girl alone." Mo picked up his hat to leave,. "I'll holla at you tomorrow. Remember what I said and leave Angela alone." Mo left.

DeShun couldn't relax so he grabbed his keys and left. He didn't feel like being alone so he decided to go down to the pool hall for a few more drinks. To his surprise, Drake was the first person he saw as he entered. He decided to have one drink and make a quick exit. *I don't need any more shit tonight,* DeShun thought irritability to himself.

"DeShun, my man, what up?" Drake said in a rather cheerful mood.

"Not much," was all DeShun said hoping he'd get the hint and just leave him alone.

"I heard congratulations were in order. You and Angela are having a baby or at least you're the one she chose." Drake was smiling but it didn't quite reach his eyes. "Don't get me wrong, I was pissed when I first heard but after I did a lot of thinking I figured maybe it was a blessing because I was getting real tired of her foolishness." Drake pulled out a cigarette, "Besides she would have done nothing but get my ass locked back up, because she would have eventually made me damn-near kill her crazy ass." Drake laughed as he turned to leave then said mockingly, "You know, the more I think about it, maybe you the crazy one for messing with Angela. That ex-girlfriend of yours is awfully fine; no wonder you had to hit it one last time before you could let go."

DeShun continued to hear Drake's taunting laughter even after he had walked away. DeShun angrily paid for his drink then left, thinking he had to be crazy to have ever fucked with Angela.

Chapter Fourteen

Kayla sat drinking her whiskey-laced coffee and told Ashland all about DeShun and Angela; she didn't leave anything out and slowly she began to feel better. She also fumed how she could not, nor would she ever, forget how Damian deliberately kept Madison a secret.

"Oh, before I forget: Mom called and told me she had a surprise for me. I wouldn't be scared to bet she and your dad got engaged."

For a brief moment, Ashland smiled sadly. "I know. Dad called and told me the same thing."

"So why do you seem so gloomy?" Kayla asked her.

Ashland immediately laughed. "I'm not gloomy, I'm actually excited." Ashland called the waitress over and ordered them another drink. "Kayla, Damian loves you, why don't you sit down and talk to him?"

Kayla knew something was up with Ashland when she changed the subject, but she let it go. "I don't, know it's kind of hard to admit you're jealous," she joked weakly as she rubbed her temples.

Ashland sat back and laughed.

"What are you laughing about?" Kayla inquired.

Ashland smiled. "I never thought I'd hear you admit to being jealous. You know you should just go home and work it out."

Kayla rolled her eyes at Ashland as she sipped her drink.

"Or you could leave his ass alone. Who knows what else he may be lying about or keeping from you? But then again, a rich, fine man like that, hmph, Madison would probably love to get him back." Ashland added while laughing, "Or you could just keep him, because if he's anything like his brother, his ass ain't anything but pure, raw male sexuality."

"You're just hot in the ass, that's why your lil' ass has been pregnant for two years straight," Kayla joked as she stood and placed money on the table.

"Where are you going?" Ashland asked.

"I need to go talk to my man before some tramp like you tries to steal him away," Kayla said pulling Ashland to her feet and they laughed all the way out the door. Kayla still wondered what had made Ashland so sad earlier when she'd spoken of their parents.

***

Before Kayla could insert her key in the door, Damian opened it looking sexy and rugged with his shirt half way unbuttoned. He leaned against the door in such a way Kayla thought he was not going to let her in. "Where you been?" He asked.

"With Ashland, do you plan on letting me in? We really need to talk," she said to him.

Damian stared at Kayla intently for a moment before stepping aside for her to enter. He led the way outside onto the kitchen deck. He stopped only to refresh his drink. He sat down and took a long swallow. "Now what is it we need to talk about?" Damian questioned her with stormy unreadable eyes.

Kayla was taken aback by the fiery glare he was giving her. "Why are you looking at me like that?"

Damian laughed as he took another swallow. "Are you trying to play me for a fool?"

Kayla sat dumbfounded because she had no idea what he was talking about. She knew they had a few problems but not enough to warrant the look he was giving her. Right now he looked as if he simply despised her. "Is this a bad time? Maybe it would be better if we talk later."

Kayla was beginning to feel uncomfortable with him looking so violent and knew something had to be seriously bothering him.

Even though Damian knew he needed to quit drinking, he leaned back in his chair and casually took another swallow. "No. Now is fine. Let's be straight up with each other. I love you, but I won't tolerate you and your ex sneaking around behind my back."

Kayla frowned. "What are talking about? Are you drunk or what? I told you there has been nothing between us for a long time now."

Damian laughed cynically. "Yeah, that's what you said, isn't it?" Damian stood abruptly, "On second thought, maybe you're right, it might be best if we talk later."

Kayla sat as she watched him walk away. She was at a complete loss because she had no idea what he was talking about or why he was so angry. Then it finally occurred to her he may have possibly seen DeShun kiss her earlier today. She found Damian in their bedroom taking his shirt off as he prepared to shower. He stood completely still staring at her, silent and unreadable.

"I love you," Kayla began as she slipped off her sandals, "I don't want anyone but you. No man has ever made me feel the way you do." She slowly removed her shirt and pants. "I mean, you do such amazing things with your hands." She unsnapped her bra. "Then that wonderful mouth of yours makes me tingle just by looking at it." She slid her panties off teasingly. "Then there is that powerful tool of yours that makes me absolutely dizzy with so much unadulterated pleasure." She began walking toward the bathroom. "I'm simply hooked on you and there is nothing nor is there anyone out there for me but you. Don't make me wait too long." Kayla turned the shower on and prayed he would join her.

***

Kayla had no idea how long they stayed in the shower but the cold water forced them to end their tryst. Damian sat down beside her and tenderly kissed her on her forehead. She wanted to confide in Damian about everything, but right now, she couldn't. As crazy as it sounded she couldn't because she was more afraid of the reaction she would get after she told him that she didn't call the police on DeShun today.

And then the idea of becoming completely dependent upon another man was beginning to make Kayla nervous; she didn't want to be hurt again. She also wondered if he had any feeling left for Madison even though he had assured her Madison was his past. Kayla knew Damian was different but she didn't want to end up making the same ol' mistakes. She also didn't think she was strong enough to lose him completely for any reason, which she knew might happen if they weren't completely open and honest with each other. "DeShun stopped by today," Kayla began.

Damian sat quietly and stared at Kayla for a long moment then stood. She knew he was more than likely teed off. If he wasn't, he would be after she admitted to him that DeShun had kissed her, no matter how brief it was. Before Kayla could say anything else Damian simply left the room. She sat there and wondered how in the world her life became so quickly out of control. When Damian came back into the room she was so lost in thought she hadn't even noticed until he had sat down beside her.

"Why would you keep Madison such a secret? You know I trust you and think we have something special but for the life of me I can't figure out your reasoning on not telling me about her before you took me over there. I can only hope it wasn't because you still feel something for her. I truly hope we are more than that."

"Kayla, I had no idea she would be there. I never

lied about anything. It never crossed my mind because she's just someone from my past, I swear. Since I've been with you, I haven't been with another woman. I haven't really seen her since we broke up all those years ago. I just recently found out she was in town and Jermaine is seeing her."

Kayla didn't say anything.

"Kayla, let's not make things complicated. I love the ground you walk on, but I really need you to trust me on this."

"Complicated? How am I making things complicated?" Kayla snapped.

Damian smiled and said softly, "I don't want to argue over someone from the past."

Kayla was angry because she had no clue about too much of anything from his past. "I'm not arguing." She moved intimately close to him as if she was about to kiss him then laughed softly as she whispered, "I'm beginning to wonder what else you're hiding from me. Who knows, maybe we rushed into everything too soon."

"Kayla, I never lied about anything, it just wasn't important enough to tell. Like I said, it never crossed my mind, she's just someone I went out with on occasion. Why can't you just let it go?"

Kayla didn't say anything because she knew he was right. She was only acting out of jealousy.

"Kayla, let's not start an argument. Just trust me."

Kayla still couldn't say anything.

Damian smiled and said softly, "Come on now, I'm serious, let's not let someone from the past ruin what we have."

Kayla became angry all over again. "DeShun is my past, so why don't you trust me?"

"I know nothing I ever say will erase the fact that I was not forthcoming with you, but there is nothing going on that I'm not afraid to admit to."

Kayla turned her head away when Damian spoke of trust but he gently grabbed her chin and turned her head back toward him, his eyes were angry.

"Can you say the same?" Damian asked.

The intensity of Damian's stare held Kayla silent as he spoke those words to her. She knew deep down she could trust him, but she wondered about herself. She felt so out of control since the rape, no matter how hard she tried to fool everyone around her. The panic attacks were so embarrassing she knew she couldn't tell anyone, not even Ashland. She only wondered how long she would be able to keep anyone from finding out.

After Kayla never answered him, Damian stood and left her sitting on the bed. She followed him on weak legs, and told him everything about Angela and DeShun. As soon as she stopped talking he left the room, leaving her staring at the closed door. She wanted to call him back but instead she went to their bedroom and stripped down and slid under the covers. *Why didn't I just call the police on DeShun?* Kayla began questioning herself.

Chapter Fifteen

It was difficult to walk away from Kayla because Damian knew she needed him. He wanted to hold her all night but he needed to think. After putting on a pair of pajama pants he poured another drink then went to sit out back to enjoy the evening breeze. He thought of Kayla and smiled as he imagined her fighting DeShun. He had been relieved when she had told him she was completely over him, but the idea of DeShun stealing kisses from her at his every open opportunity aggravated the hell out of Damian. He wished he had not gotten jealous and drove away. He would have loved the opportunity to give DeShun the ass-whooping he deserved.

Damian could honestly say no woman had ever caused him to get jealous to the point that he was actually bothered. Kayla had definitely affected him and become his weakness and he honestly didn't like the fact that he was feeling possessive of her. Feeling frustrated, Damian picked up the phone to call in a favor from one of his shadier friends to have him do a little research on Angela.

The next morning after Damian left for work, his friend called him with some information about Angela; to his surprise, she actually worked for one of his grandfather's smaller companies. He decided he would pay her a visit later that day.

When Damian walked into the Human Resources office, the secretary wasn't at her desk and Ted Majors, the Human Resources Director, was nowhere in sight. Damian entered the file room then began searching the files to see exactly which area Angela worked in, and to his surprise she was the secretary to this department. He replaced all the files except one, and then went out to sit at her desk to wait on her or Ted's return. She was away almost an hour and the phone rang exactly twenty seven times. Damian was not happy or impressed with this or a lot of other things he'd seen and heard since being here. He decided it was time to start 'cleaning house' as soon as he returned back to his office.

Damian heard two women talking and laughing rather loudly even before they reached him. His back was toward them as he continued to lean back reading over a few documents on her desk. When he turned around and looked up casually the taller of the two, who was dressed in a long black skirt and a grey blouse that looked two sizes too small, snatched the paper from his hand then asked, "What are you doing at my desk?" Damian had to fight the urge to fire her on the spot.

Damian leaned back further in Angela's chair as he propped his foot up on her desk. Her eyes became small but she remained silent as the other girl laughed. "Would you excuse us please?" He said to the laughing woman.

"Excuse ME?" the woman asked with sarcasm.

Damian then asked questioningly, "Do you work here?" He couldn't believe the way she was dressed, her breasts were straining against the fabric of her too short and much too tight dress.

"Yeah I do, but what's it to you?" she asked Damian haughtily while Angela eyed him suspiciously.

"Well, I would suggest you get back to work so that I may have a word with Miss Bryson," he stated calmly.

Angela and the woman laughed.

"Get out of my chair," Angela said as recognition fell over her eyes and she dismissed him while placing a coffee cup down on her desk.

Damian continued to sit, but before he could respond Ted Majors gasped loudly then stuttered nervously, "Mr.

Maxwell, oh my, we hadn't expected to see you here for a couple of weeks. Your brother had called me this morning to let me know you were now in charge of this division."

Angela and the woman looked at Damian curiously.

"Angela, JaMeka, this is Mr. Maxwell, he's the owner of this company. JaMeka you need to get back to your desk immediately," Ted said anxiously.

Upon hearing Damian was the owner JaMeka mumbled an apology then scurried quickly off. Angela looked completely shocked then turned toward Ted as he spoke. "Angela, what were you doing away from your desk?" Ted asked agitatedly.

Damian sat there wanting to laugh because Ted had been away from the office the whole time he'd been here also. Damian stood. "Miss Bryson, may I have a word with you?" Damian looked over at Ted as he continued to shift nervously where he stood. Damian would deal with him later.

Angela only nodded then led the way to the conference room. Damian waited until she'd sat down at the table before he leaned up against the table beside her.

"How's Kayla?" Angela asked casually before he could say anything.

Damian continued to lean against the table trying to figure her out, then just as casually he said, "considering everything that happened, she's doing fine."

"So I guess you plan on firing me? Is that what this is about?" she asked as if she didn't have a care in the world.

Damian wanted to fire her but he wouldn't, at least not yet. He'd let the 'clean up crew' handle that.

Damian ignored her question then asked, "Do you have insurance here?"

She looked completely baffled by his question. "Yes. Why you wanna know?"

"You know, the Mental Health plan is excellent, have you thought about using it?" Damian questioned boldly knowing it was bound to piss her off. "You see, Kayla has no interest in DeShun whatsoever and for you to become enraged to the point of threatening violence is a sure indication of needing some form of mental therapy." He put his hands casually in his pockets as he continued, "I really don't appreciate the way you stepped up to her at all. DeShun and Kayla are history, so why don't you do us all a favor and leave it that way?"

"By the way, let me enlighten you on one thing: When a man cheats on his woman that doesn't necessarily mean he stops loving her, and as we all know, DeShun still loves or has some feelings left for Kayla. They do have two children together. But the kicker to all of this is Kayla does not love DeShun anymore, and that's the part you're failing to comprehend. Kayla broke it off with DeShun, not the other way around. Besides, why would a woman want a man who'd rape her?" Damian spoke calmly and evenly without raising his voice as he looked closely at Angela. Damian could tell she was seething inside, but didn't care, because what she had done to Kayla had really pissed him off.

Angela leaned back and smiled. "Well since you're not going to fire me, I take it you just came to ask me to leave Kayla alone. Am I right? Oh and since you're not going to fire me would this be a good time for me to ask for a raise? The more I think about it, the more I think a raise would most definitely make me forget all about little Miss Kayla. You do want me to forget about her don't you? Oh and let me enlighten you, have you ever thought for one second maybe Kayla enjoyed the roughness from DeShun?"

Damian stood to look out the window because her careless attitude about the rape and her nerve to try and blackmail him into giving her a raise really sent him over the top. "You can do whatever you want." He told her evenly without emotion and without looking at her.

When Damian turned back around Angela was sitting on top of the table with her skirt pulled up, she was panty-less and spread eagle. "So tell me, Mr. Maxwell, do you want to sample what caused DeShun to stray from Kayla?" She licked her fingers then began fingering herself slowly.

Damian was so revolted and disgusted by her that he stepped intently toward her. "Angela, there is absolutely nothing about you that even remotely turns me on. If you want my opinion, I seriously doubt DeShun would choose you over Kayla, but I also think DeShun is the biggest fool ever to mess around with somebody like you when he had Kayla waiting for him at home."

Angela nervously jerked her skirt down as Damian took a few more steps toward her.

"Now I am not asking, I'm telling you: don't screw with me where Kayla is concerned, because if you go near her ever again with anymore of your trifling bullshit I promise you, you will regret it, because your little collection of weapons is nothing but a mere drop in the bucket to what I could have done to you." He purposely walked up to her, lightly touched her hair and whispered in her ear, "You wouldn't want to dance with the devil, now would you?" Damian stood up straight. "Then I suggest you be careful of the things you do, because I don't think you'd want to end up like your friend Marsha, now would you? Oh, don't look so surprised I know what you did to her, but that's nothing compared to what could happen to you."

Damian stepped back and walked toward the door, angry at himself for allowing her to get next to him. "Angela, be a good girl and do some work around here for a change." He left her with a startled expression on her face.

After returning back to his office and looking over

the file he had taken, Damian got in touch with the "cleaning crew," but informed them to fire Angela last and to take their time in 'cleaning house.'

Chapter Sixteen

That afternoon, Angela could hardly wait to get home. She hadn't even cared in the least when Mr. Majors told her to use a few personal days; she was more than cooperative. She couldn't help but laugh as she thought to herself how Damian's sudden appearance shook him up pretty bad. *He was just standing there looking so fucking stupid.* As soon as she walked through her front door she called her cousin Thomas Thomason, better known as Tom-Tom, and smiled as she thought of how she had informed her nosey sister that Tom-Tom's pregnant wife needed her to come down for a few days. Angela smiled. *Damian Maxwell doesn't even have the slightest idea of who he just fucked with.*

"Are you leaving today?" Madison asked.

"Yeah." Angela hoped she didn't start in on her about anything because right now she wasn't in the mood and could hardly wait until Madison's vacation was over so she would leave.

"How long are you going to be gone?" Madison asked.

"Look , Madison, I'll be gone for a few days, maybe even a week. That will give you and Mallory the house to yourselves for a change." Angela said then raised an eyebrow, *her ass has the nerve to frown.*

"Angela, how are you just going to take off from work like that? You know if you keep on messing around like you're doing you're going to end up losing your job. Then what do you plan on doing because I'm not supporting you again," Madison said with her hands on her hips.

Angela stood speechless and thought angrily. *Now*

this heifer acts as if she's my momma or something. Shit, I'm a grown- ass woman and can do what I want to do. She thinks she's all that since she got that good paying job. She best be glad Mallory ran in the room because I was getting ready to tell her ass something. Miss High-and-Mighty so secretive and won't even tell anyone who Mallory's daddy is. Shit, she got Mallory all secretive-acting too, the poor girl thinks it's normal or some kind of game to keep who her daddy is a secret. All Mallory ever tells me is his name is Daddy. Probably one of them stiff-shirts she works with cause Madison's ass thinks she's too good for anyone else. His ass is probably married with a few kids of his own, too.

"Auntie, look what I made today! See, it's a book I wrote all bound up with my picture. Miss Ruby helped me make it. You like it? I made Daddy one too," Mallory said smiling.

Angela loved Mallory because she was the only bright spot in her life. Angela just prayed her baby would be healthy and just as sweet as Mallory so she could enjoy motherhood. Angela also hoped this child wasn't bad like a lot of kids around and that she didn't get bored too quickly with it, *cause if I do DeShun will be raising this child by himself, and the damn baby might not even be his.* Angela laughed to herself.

***

Tom-Tom and his family lived in the country, and Angela swore it was the most beautiful place she had ever seen. She arrived about eight that night. After talking to his wife Lexie for a while Angela told her she wanted to chill out at the gazebo by the lake before going to bed. Angela loved it there as she thought, *Tom-Tom's house is the bomb, but all those bad-ass kids of his get on my damn nerves.*

"Angela, Angela, will you play hide and go seek with us?" Their five-year-old daughter ran up and asked.

Angela thought, *she's the cutest little thing with*

those long pigtails of hers but I do not feel like playing any games tonight with a bunch of little terrors. Angela thought they needed to be getting ready for bed and anyway, she had more important things on her mind than hide-and- seek. Angela was about to respond to her but Tom-Tom walked up.

"Pumpkin, Angela just got here and she's probably tired from the drive, why don't you go play with your brothers and sisters? She'll get a chance to play with you guys later." He leaned down and tenderly kissed the top of her head sending her on her way.

Angela smiled because no matter what Tom-Tom did out there in the streets, he was always the loving husband and father. "What's up, cuz?" Angela couldn't help smiling because she knew things were about to get started.
He sat down and asked her seriously, "You tell me."

Angela explained to Tom-Tom all the happenings in her life. No matter how Tom-Tom felt she knew in the end he'd have her back, he always did because blood was thicker than water. Right after they all graduated, she and Drake had one of their fights so Tom-Tom and Lexie took her out to try and make her feel better. They all got drunk and after dropping Lexie off, things got out of hand. Angela and Tom-Tom ended up sleeping together and Angela had always thought it was the best sex she'd ever had. It was a huge mistake but after that night, deep down, she truly regretted that Tom-Tom was her first cousin. Angela knew Tom-Tom was afraid she would tell Lexie, so to this day, she and Tom-Tom had never spoken about that night and he'd always been there for her.

"What do you want from me, Angela? I've slowed the business down a lot lately. I can't keep putting the kids and Lexie at risk anymore. Shit, I got more than enough money put away for all my kids to go to the best colleges," he said seriously.

Angela sat dumbfounded for a whole minute as she digested that information. *Cuz had paper, and shit, Lexie was pregnant with their seventh child.* "I just want to teach Damian Maxwell a lesson. All I need is some information on his family and a little money to get things started."

Tom-Tom laughed. "Every time you ask me for favors like this I always end up cleaning up your mess."

"Look, I got it this time. Come on now, help me out. I promise I won't get caught up in anything this time." Angela smiled but they both knew he was telling the truth. She always did end up calling him. She will never forget the first and the worst time she had to call him, and neither will he, because he was the one that helped her bury Marsha.

Angela really needed his help so for the very first time she decided to give him a little reminder of their past. She smiled seductively as she licked her full juicy lips and leaned in closer to him giving him a very nice, but very brief, view of her swollen ample breasts. "Come on help me out this last time, you know, for old time's sake." Angela saw a look that she couldn't figure but it somehow sent an unnerving chill though her. She laughed nervously as she tried to shake it off.

"Angela, you screw up this time I won't be there," Tom-Tom said firmly and sat back further in his chair.

"Yes, you will." Angela smiled as she stood to get ready for bed. She was satisfied but deep down she knew she had crossed the line, but the urge to make Damian suffer overpowered everything else.

By the next night, Angela was on a natural high and on her way to pay a visit to Damian's parents. Tom-Tom had come right on time first thing this morning with everything she'd asked for. *Shit, Cuz even surprised me with ten thousand dollars and chartered this flight for me under someone else's name.*

Chapter Seventeen

"The cottage is beautiful. How in the world did you manage to convince them to sell?" Carmen asked as she sank further into the hot tub and thought of her new vacation home.

"Just my charm, baby. Besides, you know once I set my sights on something I always get it." Mitchell leaned over and began kissing her.

"I think this will make the perfect spot for the kids to come to."

Mitchell frowned, "Carmen, you promised - it's just me and you for the next two weeks."

Carmen laughed, "Sorry, old habits die hard." She began kissing Mitchell passionately. "I love you so much."

"I love you too, Carmen."

Carmen frowned. "Did you hear something?"

"No, baby. It was probably-"

Whatever Mitchell was about to say died on his lips as the cottage exploded. Angela stood back and smiled as the exquisite, picturesque cottage disappeared from sight and the brilliance of the fiery lights lit up the dark sky. She hadn't meant for the explosion to be so big but laughed to herself as she thought of Damian.

Chapter Eighteen

DeShun could hardly get so lucky, he thought to himself, as JaMeka told him about she and Angela's run-in with "The Boss." Angela had actually been sent home for a few days. Things were beginning to look up and Angela hadn't even tried to see him over the past few days.

He sat at his desk and got a lot of work done for once, because lately he'd really slacked off by not being able to concentrate on anything or meeting his deadlines. By four thirty he had his desk cleaned off and was once again organized and in control. He was satisfied and happy, even when Mr. Rowland, who had replaced Mr. Majors, called him into his office.

As soon as DeShun entered Mr. Rowland's office he noticed two men dressed casually standing near the window whispering; immediately they stopped talking. DeShun was asked to sit by Mr. Rowland who introduced them. By that time, DeShun really hadn't heard too much of what was said; he was in shock and was beginning to sweat because he knew he was about to lose his job. Over the past few days people had been leaving left and right. He laughed because he had allowed Angela to get to him and jeopardize his job. Surprisingly, he didn't really feel too bad because he knew he had excellent credentials and knew he could easily trick one of his girlfriends into putting him up for a while. To his shocked surprise, he was only given a verbal warning and sent on his way; next time he would be fired, no questions asked.

DeShun should have been happy that he wasn't losing his job but he laughed instead because he had learned that he actually worked for Kayla's soon-to-be husband. He couldn't help but laugh mockingly at himself and the whole situation. *Oh well*, he thought to himself, *it is definitely time for me to start looking for another job and another place to stay before my ass gets locked up.* DeShun shuddered as he wondered why he hadn't seen Damian by now.

As DeShun was walking to his car, his cell rang. It was Mo telling him Yazmeen was found dead in her apartment. She had been found by her own son. DeShun had been shocked to learn drug overdose was suspected because in all the years he'd known her, she would never touch anything other than weed. As soon as he disconnected his call, he saw his other baby's mama, of all people, waiting for him.

"What the hell are you doing here? Why didn't you just call?" He asked annoyed as he looked around because the last thing he needed was to have Angela see them together.

"I had some things to take care of on this side of town and I forgot to charge my cell. Can we meet today? I really need to see you. Don't look like that. Our daughter is fine; she's staying the night with her cousin so I'll meet you at our usual spot in about an hour," she said then drove off without waiting for a reply.

DeShun had a good mind not to show up but he didn't want to do anything to piss her off, besides after all these years, she'd never given him any problems as long as he spent time with her whenever she was in town.

He parked his car beside hers at his great-grandfather's lake house and as soon as he walked through the door he saw her standing in the kitchen staring absently out the back door. Looking at her reminded him of when they were younger and in love. They had to keep it a secret because her parents had preferred her not to have boyfriends. They had both been virgins when they had first come here, excited and scared at the same time. This lake house had become their home away from home; every chance they had gotten they would sneak here just so they could be together.

After they graduated she caught him with one of his other girlfriends and even after he had apologized and had no intentions of cheating on her again, she slept with some guy she had met at college. That angered him to the point of them breaking up but through everything, they never stopped meeting by the lake to enjoy one another and to this day, no one ever knew about them. Well, no one except for Mo.

They continued to see other people, or at least he did, because after she broke up with her boyfriend from college he once again became her only lover. By then it was too late, he had made Angela his lover out of spite and had already met Kayla who had given him two kids. He wasn't about to give her up because Kayla had been his virgin also, *besides*, he thought to himself, *why should I have given one of them up when I knew I could have them all, then some?*

"What's up? And tell me why you all up on my job?" DeShun demanded of her.

"I missed you." She smiled seductively as she walked over to stand only inches away from him.

DeShun couldn't help it. He knew he would always be attracted to her no matter what. He may have lost Kayla, but this one would always be his. "I missed you too," he said as he slowly began to undress her.

Chapter Nineteen

Kayla couldn't sleep and it was almost midnight, so she turned on the television then jumped in the shower hoping it would relax her. *Thank goodness I took tomorrow off,* she thought to herself. As she was drying off she noticed pictures of Mitchell and Carmen flashing across the screen. She was in complete shock as she turned up the volume. They had been killed in some explosion whose source hadn't been determined yet. "Oh no!" She was shaking uncontrollably as she rushed from the room to find Damian.

Kayla didn't know how long she searched for him before she finally found him in the computer room. It was completely dark and he looked awful. She could tell he was drunk. Words were beyond her so she just took him in her arms and cried. Damian was a complete mess, understandably so, but surprisingly he never shed a tear; he only held Kayla silently as she cried.

When Kayla woke up she was alone on the sofa covered by a blanket; the clock on the wall read eight forty-seven. She searched the house but Damian was no where to be found, so she decided to pick up the few things around the house that had been left out of place. She was finished cleaning in less than thirty minutes. She checked the refrigerator to make sure they had enough food to eat. She decided she would go shopping.

Kayla thought her anger at him over an ex-girlfriend had been a little over the top. She realized they couldn't live by the past so she had to just get over it. Damian loved her and the kids and he wouldn't just turn his back on them like DeShun had done. She laughed when DeShun came to mind, *nothing but a wanna-be high baller.* Next time he came around she would definitely call the police. For safety measures, she stopped by the police department to file a restraining order against him. *His ass is probably just trying to set me up, acting all remorseful and shit just to make it seem like he never raped me.* Kayla told the detective everything she knew to help them catch him more quickly.

***

Kayla loved shopping so she bought enough food to fill their refrigerator, freezer and pantry. She was in the kitchen cooking when Damian got home. She knew she looked a mess because he was looking oddly at her. She wiped her hands on a towel and self-consciously smoothed her hair back to make sure it was still secured in a ponytail. She was embarrassed as she looked down at her stained t-shirt, cut off jean shorts and her bare toes. Kayla would have been surprised to know that Damian thought she looked quite attractive standing there. She took a deep breath and smiled. "Hey, dinner is ready."

Damian dropped his keys on the table as he took a bottle from the cabinet, sat down and began pouring himself a drink. "I'm not really hungry right now, but it smells good though."

Kayla just stood there because she really didn't know what to say. She didn't want to start an argument about his drinking on an empty stomach but she was worried about him because he really wasn't much of a heavy drinker. She did the next best thing; she grabbed a glass from the cabinet, sat down beside him and poured herself a drink. After taking a swallow she did not understand how he could drink that stuff straight but she was determined to hang in there.

"Have you eaten?" Damian asked as he watched her pour another.

Kayla hid her smile because right now he may not care about himself but she knew he cared about her. "I guess

I'm not really hungry either, maybe later."

Damian stood to see what all she had cooked. He fixed them both a small plate. Neither of them seemed to have much of an appetite but they managed to eat most of what he prepared.

"How was your day?" Kayla asked as she washed their dishes.

Damian just sat and poured himself another drink. "I got a lot accomplished." He sat quietly.

Kayla could tell he really didn't feel like talking so she sat down and poured herself another drink but made sure she put ice and coke in her glass this time. "I love you," she said.

Damian only smiled as he stood to sit outside on the kitchen deck. Kayla knew he wanted to be alone for a while so she went to take a hot shower. Damian was still outside when she returned to the kitchen to put away the uneaten food. She didn't know what to do. Her heart went out to him because she knew he was in a lot of pain and all she wanted was to take it away. She went out to sit quietly beside him and held his hand.

Damian tenderly kissed her hand then stood rubbing his chin. "Their funeral will be held in a week. That will give grandfather time to get home. We're having one funeral for both. We want to get it over with as soon as possible," Damian said quietly as he began pouring himself another drink; the bottle was empty. Damian laughed with unshed tears in his eyes. "This one's gone already and I think I might be out of brandy. Hope not because I really don't want to finish the night off with vodka. Be right back."

Kayla stood in the doorway and watched Damian take a bottle from the cabinet. He looked over at her with grief-stricken eyes and said, "I never got a chance to talk to her. You know she died knowing I was angry at her. Hell, I basically told her I never wanted to see her again. " He looked at the clear liquid then suddenly threw the bottle against the wall; it shattered on impact. At that moment, Kayla felt so much compassion and love for him that she couldn't stand to see the pain he was in. It didn't seem fair for him to lose both parents at once and it definitely didn't seem fair to Mitchell and Carmen. She went to him and held him as they sank down on the kitchen floor. The loss of both his parents finally hit him full force; hot tears and waves of anguish racked his entire body.

"She knew you loved her. Mitchell knew it also," Kayla said comfortingly.

Chapter Twenty

When Angela got back to work she discovered a lot of changes, the worst one being Mr. Majors being replaced by Mr. Rowland, who was heavily into the church. To top everything off he was a stickler for rules and regulations. *Oh well, there go my long lunches.*

As Angela swirled around in her chair, she caught a glimpse of Damian and Mr. Rowland entering the conference room. She smiled as she sat her coffee cup down on her desk then stood to go over to them. Fortunately the door was open but she still knocked politely before entering. "I'm so sorry to disturb the two of you, but I wanted to make sure to give you my deepest condolences on the loss of your parents before you left," Angela said quietly to Damian.

"Thank you," was all he said.

"Yes, that was a tragedy; you're in all our prayers," Mr. Rowland said.

Angela really didn't feel like listening to Mr. Rowland get started on any of his religious sermons and all she really wanted to do was make Damian think, so she leaned back on the table the way she did the day he spoke to her and said, "Did they ever find out what caused that massive gas leak at your parents' cottage?"

"Is that how it happened? Last I'd heard it was undetermined; I must have missed that part of it. Goodness, Son, I truly am sorry for your loss," Mr. Rowland said as he sat down.

Damian was quiet for a minute as he briefly looked hard at Angela before he became unreadable. "No, they didn't. Now if you will excuse us, Mr. Rowland and I have a few things to discuss."

Angela stood up and smiled brightly looking Damian dead in his eyes. "No problem. I'm just going to be a good girl and go do some work." She stopped at the door and said cheerfully to Damian, "Oh yeah, I almost forgot I never answered your question, you know, what you asked me last time we spoke? Yes I would." Damian frowned slightly before becoming unreadable again as Angela continued to speak, "Mr. Maxwell, I truly do love to dance." She giggled like a school girl. "Devilishly so. Oh and I took your advice and made an appointment. You know I decided to take advantage of that excellent plan you told me so much about."

"Just close the door on your way out," was all he said before completely giving Mr. Rowland his full attention.

Now that felt good knowing how he must be suffering. I bet he doesn't feel so heroic now knowing his love for one woman caused his parents' untimely demise. Oh what a harsh lesson we must learn. Angela laughed. *Oh well, I best get to work before he has Mr. Rowland fire my ass.* Angela sat at her desk and finished the rest of her coffee and began entering data into the system. She began to get a little warm so she took off her jacket. She suddenly became dizzy so she decided to walk down to the break room for ice water, but as she began descending the stairs somehow her foot slipped and she fell. Luckily, JaMeka was standing at the bottom of the stairs gossiping as usual. Angela suddenly thought how JaMeka was pretty much the only friend she had up in the place.

The fall had Angela shaken a little but she felt alright. With the baby, though, she decided it was best to just sit up for a minute before she stood to get her bearings together since no one really saw except the woman JaMeka had been talking to. Then just as quickly, JaMeka's loud, brazen voice brought everyone's attention over. Angela rolled her eyes angrily. *I would kick her stupid, country ass right here and now if I wasn't sprawled across this damn floor.*

"Shit, that looked like it hurt. Oh my God! I forgot you pregnant, girl, you alright?" JaMeka said as she helped Angela up and walked her over to a chair.

Angela was no longer embarrassed. She was pissed because she overheard a couple of comments. "I bet if DeShun had seen her fall he'd be down on his knees hoping and praying she'd lose that damn baby she's carrying." Then another person responded, "It probably isn't even his, with her nasty ass." Angela instantly thought feverishly to herself, *I wish I knew who said that shit because I'd really teach that motherfucker a lesson.*

Angela ignored JaMeka and the snickering and stood to go back to her desk. By the time she got off she was spotting and cramping pretty badly so she decided to go to the hospital. She lost her baby that night and went through it all alone because DeShun, JaMeka and not even her sister answered their phones.

Chapter Twenty-One

Damian had been working long hours at the office only taking one day off and that was the day of his parents' funeral. He thought of Jordan and their grandfather and how hard it was to tell what Jordan was feeling about what had happened. He knew his grandfather was grieving but he wondered about Jordan. Jordan wouldn't talk about it, so he figured it was his way of coping with everything, but he had grown up thinking they were dead anyway.

Kayla was working crazy hours, planning the wedding and was busy buying things for their new home before the closing, so Damian really didn't think it bothered her too much that he was hardly home. To his surprise, Kayla had asked him that morning if he regretted becoming involved with her. He had been completely shocked. He loved her and the kids, they were his family, and after she explained the whole situation concerning the kiss with DeShun he thought they were ok. He knew there still was the slight problem with Madison hanging around the office a lot lately but it was only because of Jermaine. Damian truly wished he had been straightforward about everything in the beginning.

Kayla told Damian that the kids were spending the weekend with Ashland and Jordan and that she was getting away for a few days. He did not want her to go; he knew he hadn't been there too much over the past few weeks but he had absolutely no regrets where their engagement was concerned.

"I seemed to have packed too many things," Kayla said smiling as she struggled with her overnight bag, sitting it down by the door. "You ok?"

"I will be," he told her.

"Hey," she said smiling as she kissed him, "I just need a couple of days to get my head straight."

"So why don't you just stay so we can get things straight together?" He asked.

Kayla seemed to be at a loss for words. "I just need some time that's all," she said.

"I love you and I don't want you to go," Damian told her.

"I know; I love you too." Kayla simply picked up her bag and left.

After Kayla left, Damian sat down on the couch and thought about the last few weeks. He knew he wouldn't be able to handle it if Angela did something to Kayla or the kids, especially after losing both his parents. Now he knew that Angela knew exactly what really happened to them, which was why he told Mr. Rowland to give her a raise. He wanted to throw her off and make her feel as if she was in control.

After his parents' so-called accident, the Feds told Damian not to go into any of the details while they investigated, so he, Tylen and Jordan hadn't told anyone anything, not even Kayla, Megan, nor Ashland. The only thing that was ever publicized was that the cause of the explosion was undetermined; there was never any mentioned of a gas leak or the cottage they had been staying in.

Damian laughed at himself for underestimating Angela, *which definitely would not happen again*, he thought bitterly. He would now take her very seriously and would definitely be taking care of Angela, making sure she got everything she deserved.

Damian called the investigators, but they wanted to remain tightlipped about the case so he called a friend that worked there and he gave Damian an earful, but still they had no suspects. As Damian thought of Angela, a strange calmness and determination overcame him. He knew it was nothing short of pure hatred and loathing, which he assumed was a normal feeling one gets when one discovers the person who murdered or was responsible for a loved one's death.

Damian picked up the phone to set up a meeting with his friend. After making his call he went to the kitchen to get something to drink. No more alcohol to try and mask his pain. He decided drinking bottled water would be much better because he wanted to feel the pain from the loss of his parents that way when the time came, 'handling' Angela would be easy. He went to pack his overnight bag because he was flying out to meet with his old college roommate.

***

"Damian Maxwell, how the hell have you been? Still living that carefree life on the water?" His friend asked as he stood to shake his hand and give him a hug.

Damian smiled because it was good to see someone from back in the day.

"So how's my girl, Carmen, doing? Make sure you tell her I'm old enough to take care of her now and be your daddy as well," he joked playfully as he had in the past.

Damian couldn't help clearing his throat as the usual emotional turmoil tried to surface whenever his mom came to mind. "Actually that's why I'm here. I need a huge favor, and after hearing me out if you say no, I will definitely understand." He needed a drink but he'd have water instead. He waved for the waitress.

Damian's friend studied him closely as he ordered his water.

"Damian, what's going on? How is your mom doing?" His friend asked slowly.

The waitress brought Damian's water and he almost drank the whole glass at once. "She's dead. She and my father were both killed in an explosion and it was no accident," Damian said flatly and without emotion.

"So I take it you know who did it," his friend said calmly.

Damian nodded his head as he took the last swallow of water.

"Say no more. First we'll have some lunch," Damian's friend waved for the waitress, "then you'll give me a name and go back home. I'll take care of the rest." He said everything as if they were discussing a mere business deal. At that moment Damian felt somewhat sorry for Angela because even though his friend seemed relaxed and casual he couldn't hide the angry glint of pain in his eyes.

"Oh by the way," Damian said just as casually, "don't kill her, I just want her to suffer."

Damian's friend smiled his understanding. Damian knew his friend wouldn't have given killing a second thought but Damian felt killing was definitely too good for Angela. Damian also knew by the time his friend finished with her she would wish she'd never been born.

That night when Damian got home, he found Kayla sleeping in their bed. He smiled as he settled in beside her for the night.

Chapter Twenty-Two

As soon as Kayla walked out of the house she felt strangely empty, which kind of scared her because she had been so overwhelmed by her feelings and emotions lately. The rape, DeShun, Angela, Carmen and Mitchell's death, everything had seemed to hit her all at once, but after Damian had told her he loved her and didn't want her to go, she realized Damian had been there for her throughout it all.

Kayla was scared and didn't know why, but ever since Madison showed up she had been feeling a bit insecure because that was a part of Damian he chose to keep secret even when he knew she was in town. Kayla was driving away, but now she didn't want to go. She didn't need to; she and Damian were to be married and they had to learn to deal with things together, she couldn't keep running away.

Kayla turned around and went back home. She unpacked then took a hot shower and grabbed a book to read until Damian returned home. She must have fallen asleep because the next thing she knew it was morning and the sun was shining through the windows. Evidently Damian never made it home; she trusted him so she didn't worry. Kayla put on a pot of coffee as she got ready to start her day.

Kayla had taken a few days off but decided to go to work anyway. It had been a rather slow day and she was grateful. She and Ashland had decided to go shopping afterward and had only been in the boutique about ten minutes when Angela, of all people, showed up.

"Ashland, that's Angela, the woman I've been telling you about," Kayla whispered.

"Well, let's just pretend you didn't see her," Ashland

said as she continued to check out the new arrivals.

Angela managed to find her way over to Kayla.

"Well, hello, Kayla. How have you been?" Angela asked her with a distinctive smirk.

Kayla mentally counted to ten and pretended she was one of her old friends. "I've been good, and you?"

Angela smiled as she looked at the clothing Kayla had chosen. "Wow, you have some nice pieces picked out. I bet you have all of the latest clothing. Got to look good for Damian, huh? I imagine you've easily learned how to spend his money, bet those life insurance policies were a pretty sight too." Angela paused briefly before she continued, "But then again Damian was already wealthy, so you might as well enjoy all of the perks and shop 'til you drop." Angela laughed at her own joke.

Ashland was furious when she overheard Angela's comment. "Look, why don't you just back off!" Ashland knew Kayla was angry so she grabbed her arm so they could walk off before Kayla lost control.

"You *fuck* off, bitch!" Angela said to Ashland as she grabbed Kayla by her other arm.

Instantly Kayla almost lost her balance as she jerked her arm away from Angela. Kayla had to take a calming breath to gain control. She was actually surprised at herself for not immediately swinging on Angela. "If you want a piece torn out your ass, grab me again!" Kayla retorted heatedly.

"What's wrong, Kayla, afraid of the truth, are you? I bet it turned you the hell on when DeShun *supposedly* raped you. Who knows, maybe you used that *just* to get your man," Angela laughed cynically. "Now look at you. You have it made with that rich man of yours," Angela smirked.

Kayla was livid as Angela was taking everything and twisting it, making everything seem vile and ugly. "You are the one that should be afraid, because I'm telling you for the last time if you don't stay away from me I won't be held responsible for what happens."

Angela's eyes became small. "Are you actually having the nerve to threaten me?" She laughed cruelly.

Just as Kayla was about to speak, Bianca of all the people in the world walked over, carrying her daughter, Chelsea, who was excitedly reaching for Ashland. Ashland was shocked to see her mother and sister. Kayla rolled her eyes because she couldn't stand neither Angela nor Bianca. Kayla had to admit Bianca carried herself with style and held an air of power that demanded attention.

"Hello, Ashland, it's good to see you. Kayla, it's good to see you also, I hope you're doing well. Ashland, our sweet little Chelsea spotted you from across the room then accidentally got this chocolate all over herself. Do you girls mind taking her to the ladies room to clean her up for me?" Bianca asked smiling as she set her shopping bags on the floor.

Ashland and Kayla laughed because they knew Bianca and everyone else had overheard their confrontation with Angela.

As soon as Ashland and Kayla disappeared in the ladies' room, Bianca lost all pretense of being nice. "Angela, listen I couldn't help overhearing your conversation with my daughter and Kayla and I'd like to at least show you the courtesy of giving you a little advice."' Bianca stepped closer as her voice took on an intimidating, almost sinister tone. "If you knew what was healthy for you, you would leave them both alone. I will only warn you once, after that everything else is fair game. If you mess with my daughter or even Kayla I will come after you with a vengeance. And I promise I will have no mercy."

Angela looked around contemptuously. "I don't really think there is anything in here that's worth me buying." She turned to leave then stopped as if she had forgotten something. "Oh and be sure and tell Ashland and Kayla I said goodbye." Angela sashayed out as if everything around her was beneath her. "Oh and tell Kayla to say hello to my sister for me."

Bianca frowned as she watched Angela walk away.

"Hey are you ok?" Ashland asked.

"I'm ok," Bianca told her as Ashland passed Chelsea to her.

"Damn, I can't stand that bitch," Kayla whispered so Chelsea couldn't hear as she watched Angela cross the street.

Bianca shuddered because she knew there was something about Angela that was pure evil. Bianca began to worry about Kayla and knew she needed to watch her back. She had also heard a few things in the streets about her and none of it was good. "Thanks for cleaning her up for me." Bianca smiled down and kissed Chelsea.

"Are you going to bring her over later?" Ashland asked.

"For a little while, I have to get her back to Darius by morning," Bianca said.

Kayla watched as Ashland only nodded because she knew Ashland didn't agree with the fact that her mother had given Darius complete custody of Chelsea. Then again, Kayla thought, Ashland had told her once, Chelsea would probably be better off. Kayla briefly thought of everything Ashland's mother had done to her. Yes, Chelsea was definitely better off with Darius.

Bianca turned away then stopped. "You really need stay away from that woman."

Kayla shuddered because Bianca began telling them that during the time she was seeing Samuel, Angela and her best friend got into it over Angela's boyfriend back when they were in high school. The girl had simply disappeared one day and some think Angela had something to do with it.

Kayla shuddered once again. Ashland only looked at her mom contemptuously because she had been married to her father during the time she had been seeing Samuel.

Bianca looked down at her watch as she picked up her bags. "Well, I have to be going; I promised Jacob I'd pick him up from the airport." Bianca left the store.

Ashland stared bitterly at her mother's retreating form.

      ***

Kayla got home a little before six and Damian still hadn't made it home yet. She wasn't sure if he would so she decided against cooking. She just poured herself a glass of wine and sat down at the kitchen table to gather her thoughts. Images of DeShun raping her kept flashing in her mind so she decided to pour herself something stronger. After she'd gotten herself drunk she got ready for bed.

Kayla woke up from a dream that unnerved her. She stood watching a little girl in slow motion, the little girl was so beautiful, she and Damian's child. Kayla watched mesmerized as the little girl played jump rope with her friends. The little girl suddenly waved, smiled excitedly and stopped jumping but suddenly the rope came down to trip her making her fall to her knees. The little girl looked up with a dirt smeared face as she reached her arms out as if begging someone to pick her up. The little girl suddenly frowned and began screaming "Daddy! No! Daddy, Daddy, No!" Kayla slowly turned her head and saw Damian grab his stomach as he began falling slowly to his knees. Kayla was slowly running toward Damian as he yelled, "Kayla, no, the baby!" Kayla frowned as she looked down at her stomach. Suddenly she was pregnant, and the little girl vanished, even though she could still hear her cries. She knew she had to get to Damian. She fell to her knees in front of him. He smiled and touched her stomach with his blood-stained hand. Damian suddenly frowned as the baby seemed to be reaching for him, her little arms trying to stretch through Kayla's stomach to reach him. "Daddy," they both heard from her stomach. A dark, mysterious shadow suddenly covered them, holding a knife. All Kayla heard were the tortured cries of a child.

Kayla had immediately awakened in a cold sweat to find Damian sleeping beside her. She snuggled up next to him closed her eyes and tried to go back to sleep, but the images of Damian bleeding, the little girl screaming brokenheartedly and the arms of the baby reaching for him, kept her awake for hours.

Chapter Twenty-Three

DeShun decided to spend a day at the lake house with his other baby's mama. He had called her cell as soon as he woke up and told her he wanted them back and if she wanted the same she knew where she could find him. DeShun had no doubt she'd show up. He had quit his job because he didn't trust Damian and also because he had a very promising job interview earlier that morning.

This week had been very uplifting because DeShun hadn't heard too much from Angela and a few days ago, JaMeka had told him Angela had lost the baby. He knew it was wrong but words could not describe how he felt when he heard this and he made a vow never to touch Angela again. *Shit, I never should have touched her in the first place.*

He thought about everything he'd been through over the years and realized he needed to get his life and priorities in order. All the women weren't necessary and his daughter and her mother needed him - and he needed them. It was time they grew up and stopped hiding out at this lake house. He did feel bad about Tymera and D'Neko because he was never there for them the way he should have been but at least they have Damian now, he thought to himself.

"Hey, baby, I made it. I had to take care of something." She placed her bag on the table and kissed him.

DeShun pulled her down on the couch with him. "I'm glad you're finally here, we need to talk," he said smiling.

"Ok but first," she kissed him and began unbuttoning his shirt, "I want you to know I am sorry Angela lost her baby, but in a way I can't help being relieved."

"I don't want to talk about Angela right now. That's history. I want my two favorite girls to move in with me," he said.

She laughed, "Who, me or Kayla?"

"Don't be like that; you know Kayla and I have been over for a long time besides she's getting married soon. You also know I'm just waiting for everything to cool down with her accusing me of raping her. I really wish she'd stop lying on me the way she's doing." DeShun knew he was wrong to keep denying the fact that he had raped Kayla, but he felt it really wasn't anyone's business. "But I did quit my job today. It hurt my ego too much to know I was working for her future husband," he said. "Besides you and I both know you've always been there even when I was with her."

"Yes and I also know, because you made sure to make it perfectly clear, that you loved Kayla and I wouldn't be around if I'd cause any trouble for the two of you," she said.

"We're over and I'm over her. I'm single and available. Do you still want me?" DeShun asked her seriously.

She took a deep breath and stared at him for a minute, he almost thought she was going to say no.

"Yes," she said softly then they began kissing. "I love you, DeShun."

"I love you too, Madison." As soon as the words left DeShun's mouth the door flew open and Madison gasps as Angela stood there with her hair flying around her shoulders like some wild, demonic being ready to do battle. DeShun was immediately reminded of the day she welded that knife so close to his manhood. He swallowed as he tried to fight the nervousness and uneasiness that he suddenly felt.

"You nasty-ass whore, you know how I feel about DeShun! How could you have done this?!" Angela raged.

Madison stood. "Angela, I am so sorry. I never meant to hurt you and I didn't mean for you to find out this way, but DeShun and I have been together on and off since high school."

Angela turned her head toward DeShun. "You bastard!"

"Yeah, I guess I am," he laughed at the truth. He also laughed because all nervousness was gone as he realized he was finally free of Angela and all of her crazy shit.

"DeShun, stop. She's still my sister. Don't be like that toward her," Madison said frowning.

"I do not need you taking up for me. And as far as I'm concerned, you're not my sister," Angela yelled.

"Why is that, Angela? I didn't do anything to you. Besides you and I both know we're not the only ones DeShun's been sleeping with over the years. We've all slept with other people. Look, Angela, I'm not trying to sound callous or anything but I was with DeShun even when you and Drake started dating; I just didn't let anyone know because of Daddy and Momma," Madison said calmly.

DeShun could tell Angela was on the verge of losing it and he wasn't about to interfere. *Shit, Angela's crazy ass probably had a knife or something*, DeShun thought apprehensively. "Angela, why don't you just leave and Madison will talk to you when she gets home."

"Why don't you fucking leave! I bet you didn't know she was seeing Jermaine Sanders, did you?" Angela was outraged. "Just another member of Damian's extended family."

DeShun was trying his best to be nice. He had to take a deep breath before calmly saying, "Angela, stop lying. Madison is not seeing anyone right now, isn't that right?" He waited on Madison's reply.

Madison grabbed DeShun's arm and said, "Jermaine

and I are just having fun that's all. There is no love involved; he doesn't want that kind of relationship. Just go on home, and I'll explain everything when I get there. I'll lock up here after Angela and I get finished. Mallory and I will be over later. We'll stop by the store and bring something to eat." She tugged his arm gently then added, "Please, DeShun."

Angela's eyes became angrier at the mention of Mallory, but when she spoke she sounded calm. "Is Mallory your daughter?"

Angela questioned DeShun and for the first time he felt like the true dog that he was for coming between two sisters this way. "Yes. Mallory is mine," he told her honestly.

"And you had the nerve to get me pregnant," Angela said furiously.

Angela's holier-than-thou attitude only pissed DeShun off. "Angela, you're standing there acting like you're the shit or some school-girl virgin that I'd molested or something. Shit, your ass is sluttier than a ho on crack. Reality check: Maybe you should have kept taking your birth control, or aborted it like you did Drake's baby. More than likely you got pregnant on purpose so it's really your own damn fault. Shit, it probably wasn't even my damn baby. And your ass probably didn't know who the father really was."

Madison became frustrated. "DeShun, go home please and I'll talk to you later."

DeShun laughed because Madison was always diplomatic and had to keep the peace. He never could figure out how two people could be so completely different even after being raised in the same environment. He looked down at Madison before he kissed her and thought how he was going to teach her a good lesson for her involvement with Jermaine. Just to piss Angela off he kissed Madison again, this time he made the kiss last longer.

"You know she likes to suck dicks, DeShun. Does Jermaine taste as good as he looks?" Angela laughed.

Madison's eyes only widened in shock. DeShun just smiled because he knew he was really going to get Madison straight once and for all.

Angela watched as DeShun picked up his keys and left. Madison followed suit by grabbing her keys and bags then saying they could talk outside. Angela took a deep breath and followed Madison out. Angela knew the thoughts she was having were wrong, because Madison was her younger sister, but she wanted to beat her to the ground. Angela took another calming deep breath.

"Angela, I'm really sorry. I guess I was wrong for not saying anything but DeShun and I've been together for so long and from day one we've always kept it a secret. I guess I just didn't know any other way to have a relationship with him. Besides you and Drake are still sleeping together."

"Forget Drake. Were you with DeShun when I lost my baby?" Angela asked.

Madison hesitated. "Yes, I was, but if I had known you were at the hospital I would have been there."

"If you'd answered your phone you would have known. What happened? Did he tell you not to answer? He probably did because I called his phone too. Tell me, Madison, did the two of you laugh about me?"

"Look, I admit I should have answered your call, but we never laughed about you. We never really talked about you," Madison said.

"Really, why is it that when, as you informed me you dated him first, you wouldn't question him about sleeping with your sister? I would have." Angela was trying her best to understand.

"Angela, when you and DeShun got together I was

with Jarvis and I hadn't cared at the time that DeShun was seeing anyone. Yeah I admit we still messed around and all, truth be told we never stopped, but I hadn't really cared, so I never questioned him about anything and he never questioned me. Later he hooked up with Kayla and I figured you had left him alone by then."

"What about when you and Jarvis broke up? I was with him then," Angela asked her.

For some reason Madison became angry. "Jarvis?" Madison laughed, "Angela, why do you think Jarvis and I broke up?"

"I remember you saying something about him cheating on you when he went on some trip with his frat brothers," Angela reminded her.

"That was part of it. You see, after I caught Jarvis cheating for the second time I was fed up. He begged me to stay with him," Madison said as her eyes became angrier as she spoke, "I found out about you sleeping with him. He bragged about it on campus, so forgive me, sister dear, if I didn't confide in you where my love life was concerned."

That caught Angela by surprise. She didn't know Madison knew. "Well, sorry about that," Angela told her.

'Sorry about that,' Madison mimicked Angela then laughed, "Is that all you have to say?"

"What do you want me to say? As you so lightly informed me about DeShun, we both also know we weren't the only ones Jarvis messed with either," Angela told her.

"Angela, you messed with Jarvis knowing full well he was my boyfriend, but I never messed with Drake or any other man you dated. I could have had Drake though, it's not like he never tried," Madison said.

"What do you mean?" Angela asked angrily. Because Madison was a little too smug, Angela felt herself becoming angry again in spite of the fact that Madison was right; she had messed with her boyfriend.

"Come on, Angela, we both know Drake cheated on you every chance he got. I was probably the only girl that turned him down, and I'm glad I did because we both know who's really responsible for Marsha's disappearance after she messed with him, don't we? That drove you crazy," Madison said angrily then added, "Well, that's beside the point and way too far in the past to dredge up. I've got to go so we'll talk later. DeShun's waiting."

Fuck DeShun. Now how is she gon' say some shit like that then expect to just leave? How the fuck did she know about Marsha? Angela wanted to know, but part of her was afraid to ask. *I just hope her ass hasn't told anyone, especially DeShun.* Angela calmed herself because if DeShun knew, he would have said something by now. Angela just couldn't figure out how Madison could be with him knowing all the women he'd had. Madison was the one with the high standards where men were concerned.

"Madison," Angela grabbed her arm and stopped her, "How could you want to be with DeShun after everything?" Angela needed to know. "Besides, Jermaine is a better pick, at least you would know he would still have a job after a few months. DeShun is not that reliable."

"I guess the same way you would be with him. I love him; always have, always will. The only difference between you and me is we have a child together and despite the fact that part of him still cares for Kayla, he knows he can't have her and he loves me. I guess we have too much history together for me to just walk away. Besides, he's sexy as hell," Madison said smiling as she began walking away.

"I fucked Jermaine," Angela told her vindictively.

"I know. I saw you two together that's why when he hollered at me, I hollered back," Madison said viciously then continued to walk away.

At that moment, Angela hated Madison with every fiber of her being. She hated her because DeShun loved and wanted her, she hated her because Jarvis had loved and wanted her, she hated her for getting with Jermaine, but most of all she hated her because Drake had actually wanted her. Madison has the perfect job, the perfect child. She was always Miss Perfect, was always a straight-A student and never got into any trouble. Angela was furious. *If only Momma and Daddy had found out about her and DeShun like they found out about me and Drake. I got a good mind to send her to Momma and Daddy.*

Angela picked up a rock and quickly caught up with Madison. She hit her and watched as Madison slowly collapsed. She watched the blood trickle through Madison's hair. Angela calmly took off her jacket and placed it under Madison's head to keep the blood from seeping to the ground. Angela ran to her car and pulled it closer to Madison as she struggled to get her in the trunk. Angela carefully placed a plastic bag under Madison's head to keep the evidence from her car. She even cleared the ground of any tell-tale signs of foul play. Now she didn't know what to do. She called Tom-Tom.

After Angela explained everything to Tom-Tom he told her to go home and act as if everything was fine. At first she had been scared because Madison was her sister, but after she convinced him it had been an accident, he decided to help her out. He told her to ask him no questions and pretend as if she and Madison left the lake house at the same time. Just stick with that story, Tom-Tom had said firmly, if she was asked or questioned by anyone.

Chapter Twenty-Four

Damian woke up to find Kayla snuggled up next to him. He wanted to make love to her but she was sleeping so peacefully he didn't want to disturb her. He just kissed her softly on her forehead before easing out of bed. They had plenty of time to be together, he thought with a smile. After showering he called Jordan to let him know he was taking the day off. He began cooking breakfast.

"What smells so good?" Kayla asked standing wrapped in nothing but a towel.

Damian's hunger for food dissipated as a new hunger took over. "You," he said quietly as he turned the stove off and walked slowly toward her and undid her towel. He began to slowly kiss and touch every inch of her delectable body right where they stood.

"Damian…" Kayla began as she trembled.

"Shhh, don't talk, don't even move. Just close your eyes and enjoy," he told her slowly as he continued to nibble away at her body. Kayla's legs began to shake so he picked her up and placed her on the couch, but as he looked down at her he couldn't take it any longer. He removed his pants and entered her slowly. He cursed to himself because he hadn't thought to get a condom, but as he pulled away Kayla stopped him.

"What's wrong?" Kayla asked in a breathless whisper.

Damian had to clear his throat before he could speak. "I need to get a condom. I'll be back."

"Don't stop please. You feel so good," she begged while gyrating her hips in a steady, mind-boggling rhythm.

Damian lost all control. He began kissing Kayla as

he grabbed her voluptuous hips and began moving within her.

***

Kayla had just left for work when the phone began ringing, it was Damian's friend. He stepped out on the balcony to talk.

After Damian's conversation he stood there thinking of what his friend had just told him. Evidently, Angela was more unstable than he thought; she had actually killed or tried to kill her own sister and had taken her body to her cousin Thomas Thomason.

His friend had sounded confident when he told Damian he had control of the situation, he'd said he knew Tom-Tom and would personally have a little chat with him. Damian laughed because he also knew of Tom-Tom's reputation, but what he hadn't known was that Angela was his first cousin. Blood is blood and that definitely was going to be one hell of a long chat.

Chapter Twenty-Five

It was good seeing a face from the past, but Tom-Tom sat back disgusted at what he was hearing. He knew Angela wasn't any good, but he didn't realize how crazy she really was. He always thought Marsha had been a jealous mistake, but after Angela killed that couple he thought about everything. Angela had planned out each incident. He didn't want to face the fact that she had deliberately hurt Madison because there was a line you simply didn't cross. Blood was blood but Angela had quickly changed the rules of the game.

"Don't worry, Madison is safe and I'll definitely take care of Angela myself." Before Tom-Tom could say another word, Lexie rushed through the door.

"Tom-Tom, come quick. Madison is dead. I don't know what happened; I left the room to get her lunch and when I got back, there was a pillow lying on the floor," Lexie said shaking uncontrollably.

Tom-Tom pulled out his radio, "I want this place on lockdown now!" He yelled. Lexie was holding her stomach so he began to worry about her. "Sit down and calm down before you go into labor. I'll take care of this." After getting Lexie settled he motioned for his friend to follow him.

After gathering his men together for questioning, Tom-Tom still knew nothing, except for the fact that McCray, who was one of his main men, was acting slightly off. After dismissing everyone, Tom-Tom asked McCray to meet him at the field house.

"You got them coming from everywhere," his friend said laughing.

"Hey, you know how it is," Tom-Tom smiled even

though he felt the loss of Madison. He even felt the loss for Angela because he would be putting the word out for no one to touch her. *I want to deal with her my damn self, if I find out for sure she killed Madison. She'll regret she ever fucked with me.* Tom-Tom was angry and that wasn't good because he needed to keep a level head.

"You think he knows something too, don't you?" his friend asked knowingly.

"Yeah," was Tom-Tom's only response, because what was about to take place hadn't happened in a long time. He wanted to give up this life but with Lexie and the kids it was hard. He had to keep a few men around just for their protection and each man knew he would settle for nothing less than complete loyalty.

"You want me to handle it for you?" Tom-Tom's friend asked.

Tom-Tom wanted to say yes because he was tired of everything but he couldn't, this was personal.

His friend continued smoothly, "I know this is family business but after everything we've been through I consider you part of my family. Let me handle it that way. If anything should come down you'll still be here to take care of Lexie and the kids."

***

After they arrived in the field house, Tom-Tom sat back in his chair as he watched his friend question McCray. His friend was smooth yet relentless and unyielding in his questioning. McCray was very nervous and sweating profusely.

McCray stood abruptly and his chair slid back crashing against the floor. "Look, I didn't know she would kill her. She said she needed to see her sister, I told her you wasn't allowing anyone access to the house for a few days but..." McCray was embarrassed as he continued, "...she, um, convinced me to sneak her in."

His friend only stared hard at McCray quietly waiting on him to continue.

"I promised not to tell she was here and in return she gave me some head and a few other things," McCray said guiltily as he turned towards Tom-Tom. "I swear I didn't think she would kill her own sister. I figured she only wanted to see Madison to make sure she was alright."

Tom-Tom rubbed his face as he thought about what to do. McCray was only being a man and he knew first hand how persistent and convincing Angela could be where sex was concerned. But he paid McCray's salary and his first priority should have been to him. "Go back to your post," Tom-Tom told him.

McCray looked worried and hesitated slightly before leaving the room. Tom-Tom's friend nodded his head slightly in understanding as their eyes locked.

Chapter Twenty-Six

DeShun sat waiting on Madison for hours because out of the blue, Madison's cousin, Miss Ruby, called him worried because Madison didn't pick Mallory up. He could only smile as he remembered Mallory's angelic apology about having Miss Ruby call him, but Madison had told Mallory to call her father if she ever felt something was wrong. DeShun had to admit he was worried because it wasn't like Madison to just forget about Mallory. He knew something was up.

"Daddy, why didn't Mommy pick me up?" Mallory asked DeShun the next morning as they sat on the sofa.

"Give me a few minutes and I'll be right back." He kissed his daughter on top of her head as he headed toward the bathroom to clean himself up so he could get breakfast started. He didn't even remember when he fell asleep last night, all he remembered was repeatedly dialing Madison's cell number and everyone he could think of with the exception of Angela. He did not feel like being bothered with her.

After breakfast and getting Mallory cleaned up, she and DeShun went shopping to pick her up a few things then they headed to the park. As he sat on the bench and watched her play with the other kids, he thought of Mo. Mo always knew what was going on so he decided to give him a call but just as he was pulling out his cell, it rang.

"Mo, what's up? I was just getting ready to call you," DeShun said.

"DeShun, you ain't gon' believe what I just heard. Madison's dead; they say she was attacked at some shopping center. But get this: Tom-Tom's involved somehow." Mo remained silent for a minute. "But word on the street is Tom-Tom's looking for Angela, and when he find her it ain't good. Some say Angela had something to do with Madison's death."

DeShun sat numb and unmoving as he listened to Mo. He watched his beautiful little girl running around with the other kids not knowing her mother was now forever gone. DeShun took a deep breath. "Mo, let me hit you up later." He hung up without hearing Mo's goodbye. DeShun didn't know how long he sat there but the next thing he knew Mallory was beside him wiping his tears away. All he could do was pick her up and hug her tight before walking them to his car. DeShun didn't know how or where he'd find the words to tell Mallory about her mother.

All afternoon DeShun struggled to find the words to explain Madison's absence to Mallory, but he was at a complete loss. He sat unmoving after getting Mallory to bed. After downing a half a beer his doorbell rang and to his surprise it was Tom-Tom.

"DeShun," Tom-Tom said stone faced.

DeShun moved aside for him to enter.

"How's Mallory doing?" Tom-Tom asked.

DeShun wondered how Tom-Tom knew Mallory was here, but there was not too much Tom-Tom didn't know. "She's fine," he told him as he sat down on the couch.

Tom-Tom sat back and stared hard at DeShun for a long minute. "Have you told her about her mother yet?"

"No," DeShun said quietly.

Tom-Tom made a scathing sound. "Madison's death is ultimately your fault, but I'm guessing you realize that by now, or at least you should. See, this is what happens when you screw around with two sisters; shit gets real ugly." From the tone of Tom-Tom's voice, it was as if he had slapped DeShun. Tom-Tom's face was unreadable which made DeShun nervous and very uncomfortable. He had enough sense to remain silent in fear of saying something to offend him.

Tom-Tom raised an eyebrow. "What are your plans?"

DeShun frowned not knowing what he was talking about.

"What do you plan on doing?" He rephrased slowly.

With Tom-Tom, DeShun knew it could cost you if you didn't handle your business, especially where kids were concerned. He felt as if he couldn't breathe as he cleared his throat and answered him. "Take care of my daughter, of course."

Tom-Tom sat studying him, as if debating. "You're nothing but a piece of shit. I never have liked you." Tom-Tom's face held a look of contempt. "I never knew what Madison saw in you. Angela, well, everyone knows she'll mess with anything." Tom-Tom leaned forward and laughed but it never reached his eyes. His eyes only held a look so hard, smothering and cold that it kept DeShun frozen where he sat. "Don't treat Mallory like you do your other kids. You better take real good care of her or I will, because Madison paid the ultimate price for loving your sorry ass. Because of you, Angela killed her own sister."

Before Tom-Tom could say another word Mallory stepped in the room with tears filling her eyes. "Daddy, what did you do to make Auntie Angela kill my mommy?"

DeShun could not respond, as hard as he tried he couldn't. The guilt which he had never really allowed himself to feel, came crashing down upon him just as he spoke those words. He didn't know what to say. After a minute he finally found the strength to stand and walk toward his daughter, but she stepped away. "Mallory come here," he heard himself practically pleading to his little girl. She looked innocent as she pouted trying to hold back her tears that he almost lost it. He could not do that, especially not in front of Tom-Tom. He got down on one knee, "Mallory, I only loved your mommy more. Baby, I love you so much. Come here." Mallory came into his arms and cried herself to sleep. Tom-Tom sat quietly watching everything.

After DeShun returned to the room from putting Mallory back to bed, Tom-Tom stood and stared levelly into his eyes without wavering or flinching. "I came here to kill you and take Mallory with me, but I can see that she needs you right now. Take care of her and everything will be cool. I'll be watching and waiting for you to slip up because nothing would give me more pleasure than putting one right between your eyes." Tom-Tom left quietly.

DeShun took an unsteady breath and went to lock the door on shaky legs. "He actually came here to kill me," he said out loud and went to the kitchen to pour himself a very large, stiff drink.

Chapter Twenty-Seven

Angela screwed up really bad. *Damn, DeShun.* She couldn't go home so she did the next best thing. She withdrew all of her money from her checking and savings accounts and decided to lay low for a while. She knew she was at the point of no return so she decided she'd take care of everyone that had pissed her off. If she got caught she knew she'd probably get life in prison for what she'd done to Madison alone, so she decided she might as well take care of all of her enemies and make it worth it. Angela started making her Death Wish List.

After completing her list she felt good, but she was indecisive as to who would go first. She decided to treat herself to a fabulous dinner first at the restaurant where she was staying then make her decision. *Dinner had been delicious,* she thought to herself as she sat at the bar to have a couple of drinks and weigh her options on who to visit first.

Angela noticed a lady sitting on the other end of the bar kept trying to make eye contact with her, she was very attractive with full lips, *but I ain't a fucking dyke.* Angela stood to walk outside to get some fresh air. She hadn't had sex in a few days and she was horny as hell; she needed to find her a man. She didn't care who as long as he was at least half way decent-looking and clean. She stood leaning against the railings sipping her drink as she watched all the couples pass by.

"Enjoying the evening breeze I see." Angela heard the calm, smooth, masculine voice coming from behind her.

Angela turned around only to come faced with a tall, dark-skinned, well-dressed and very well-built man. He was sexy beyond words in a thuggish sort of way. His hair was very low cut, almost bald, and he had thin sideburns with a manicured beard. She was becoming excited just looking at him, her panties instantly soaked from anticipation. She couldn't help but smile.

"Excuse me for being forward but I'm quite taken by your loveliness." He held out his hand for her to shake.

Angela noticed his hands were well groomed and that really turned her on. He took her by surprise so all she could think to say was thank you. She held onto his hand longer than necessary as she openly eyed him up and down. She could already imagine herself licking her tongue up and down his shaft. Angela inhaled deeply to slow down her thinking, *I want to fuck him right here and now, not even caring about us having an audience.*

He smiled as he looked at her. He had eyes made for the bedroom. "So tell me, are you here for the medical convention?" He asked Angela.

Angela wanted to laugh because she'd never thought about going into the medical field but she was pretty good with a knife. "Actually I am." The lie rolled smoothly off her tongue. "I'm a nurse, and I work for a small doctor's office over in Alabama." She smiled but she wanted to laugh because she'd never even been to Alabama. She finished off her drink. "I have a bottle of champagne up in my room if you care to join me."

"I'd like that," he whispered. Then his cell rang. "Would you excuse me please?" He said walking a few feet away.

A chill swept through Angela's body at the mere thought of having that man inside of her. Her pussy lips were throbbing and swollen so bad from excitement that the slightest movement was pure pleasure for her.

"Sorry about that. Can I get a rain check for later? There is something I've got to take care of. It shouldn't take any more than a couple of hours."

Shit, Angela couldn't help but think. "Sure," she said showing her disappointment.

"I have an idea, how about I join you later tonight?" He asked.

"Okay, I'm in room 418. I have to go out myself but I should be back before midnight." Angela told him as she pulled a business card from her purse, "Call me." Angela always kept business cards with just her name and number on it for these types of situations. She wanted him and she'd have him sooner or later, besides there was a chance she'd get too busy to get back by midnight.

"I'll be there," he said as he lightly rubbed her cheek before walking away.

"Damn, his ass is fine," Angela mumbled to herself. She could not wait a few hours but he looked to be worth the wait. *Oh well,* she thought, *I guess I'll go change my clothes and get started on my list.* Angela stopped by the ladies room before heading to the elevator. As she was coming out of the stall the woman from the bar was standing in front of the door blocking her way. "Do you mind?" Angela asked with attitude.

"I don't mind at all," The woman said and once again Angela's eyes went to her full lips as she licked them slowly. The woman gently shoved Angela back into the stall, pulled her dress up and went down on her knees.

Angela had never done anything like this before and the idea repulsed her. Angela knew she should knock that woman's ass through that door, but the woman started fingering her so expertly and when the woman pushed her tongue into Angela's already swollen pussy, she couldn't help but think of the man she'd just met. Angela imagined him licking and teasing her clit and then she imagined him sliding his big, hard penis into her waiting pussy and thinking of that made her cum instantly. Angela felt sick as she looked down at the woman she'd just let eat her out. *Nasty- ass bitch*, Angela quickly pulled her gun from her purse and hit the woman across her forehead. "I can't stand dykes," Angela said as she hit the woman repeatedly just because she had made her feel so good. Angela stood and looked down at the bloody woman and took a deep breath. "Nice hotel, but it's check out time for me. Good thing I gave him my number."

***

Angela arrived at the house as soon as she cleaned herself up. She posted up outside. The house was completely dark and there seemed to be no movement inside. She snuck around back and put tape on the window so when she broke it, it would keep the noise down. She had to adjust to the darkness as she stood in the living room and pulled out her knife.

Angela walked slowly toward the bedroom and eased the door open. He was lying there so peaceful and sexy that she couldn't help but smile. She tiptoed toward his bed and that's when she saw his eyes open. "Hi, baby," Angela whispered softly as she rammed the knife deep in his belly. That's when she heard it, a child crying for her daddy. Angela stood unmoving.

Mallory instantly stopped crying and started screaming as she looked at DeShun, "Daddy, no! Daddy, no!! Auntie Angela, please don't take my daddy too!!" Mallory screamed as she ran to her daddy with her hands held out.

Angela was so shocked to learn Mallory was there that she could only pull her knife from DeShun and step back. DeShun groaned painfully.

"You're better off without him," Angela told Mallory as she quietly left the house.

Chapter Twenty-Eight

Damian sat drinking his bottled water as he listened to his friend. His friend confirmed that Angela had definitely killed Madison and Damian felt the loss.

"I didn't think Angela would hurt Marlene but as I watched the paramedics take her away, I regretted ever getting her involved by having her distract Angela while I checked out Angela's room. Despite the fact that Marlene is a prostitute, she is a nice person and didn't deserve what happened to her," Damian's friend told him as he pulled something from his pocket. "I found this in the ladies room." He handed it to Damian.

Damian frowned. "What is this, Death Wish?" He laughed as he handed his friend the paper back. "Don't worry about me. I can take care of myself."

"I'm not. I'm just making you aware," his friend said as his cell phone rang. "Hello." His friend stood quietly as he held the phone to his ear, "We'll be there."

When Damian's friend looked at him he became unreadable. "DeShun is at the hospital in surgery as we speak and it doesn't look good. Mallory is there also. One of his neighbors heard her screams and called the police."

"Who is Mallory?" Damian asked frowning, the name sounded familiar but he couldn't place it.

Damian's friend's face became unreadable as he spoke, "Madison and DeShun's daughter, or so we thought. Angela stabbed DeShun and it looks as if Mallory cut her foot pretty bad on glass from the window Angela broke. Well, as it turns out, Mallory's blood type doesn't match DeShun's and even if it did, he wouldn't have been able to give blood. He's already lost too much." He looked unwavering at Damian. "That leaves you."

Damian sat there digesting his words. "That leaves me what?" He had to ask but he already knew the answer.

"You need to take a paternity test, but from what Tom-Tom says you were the only guy during that time he remembers Madison being with, other than DeShun," his friend said but his words seemed incomprehensible to Damian.

Damian stood to pour himself a drink because he really needed a shot of liquor but all he found was a little wine. "Alright, let's go do this," Damian said as they left for the hospital. Damian instantly thought of Kayla and wondered how she would react to this news.

***

Damian's friend sat with him as he waited on the results. After what seemed to be hours the doctor came over with the news. Damian informed the doctor it was fine for his friend to be present as he was told the results.

"Mr. Maxwell, it looks as if you're not the father either."

Damian felt bad for the little girl but he could not begin to explain how relieved he was to hear this news.

After Tom-Tom left the hospital, Damian and his friend stood in the parking lot talking for a few minutes. "Alright, well, continue to keep me informed on what's happening," Damian told him as his friend started up his car.

"Will do," he said then drove away.

Damian's car was only a few feet away, but before he reached it his Uncle Samuel pulled up. "How are you doing?" He asked.

Damian only shook his head because Samuel was the last person he wanted to see right now.

"Damian, wait a minute please. Give me one minute," Samuel said.

Damian deliberately looked down at his watch then back up at him.

Samuel laughed. "Alright. Have you ever wondered why I took your marina the way I did?" He asked.

If Samuel had been standing he swore he would have hit him, but he only looked down at his watch.

"Look, Madison confided in me years ago telling me Mallory might be your daughter. I knew DeShun wasn't that child's father, but she was in love with that man, so I said nothing. You see Madison was my daughter. My business partner and his wife were having problems and one night I was weak and began having an affair with his wife. So basically I took your marina because I was angry you'd slept with my daughter and possibly gotten her pregnant. I willed the marina to Mallory."

As Damian looked at Samuel he was completely speechless, because that would make Madison his first cousin. Although Mallory really wasn't his daughter, he'd slept with and had a relationship with his very own cousin. All he could do was walk away. After losing his parents, the marina was a part of his past and it didn't seem as important to him anymore; he really hadn't thought of it since their death. He was content working with Jordan in their family companies the way his grandfather wanted him to. Damian had even told Jordan to forget about getting the marina back.

Before going home, Damian stopped by his grandfather's house because he and Jordan had had a meeting with his grandfather earlier and he had left a file on his desk that he needed.

Tylen had recently purchased a home and had asked Megan to marry him. He was still dealing with the guilt he had about everything that had occurred with Bianca even though Ashland had assured him she wasn't angry. He still felt the need to get his own place for when he and Megan were in town, which would also give Ashland and Jordan their privacy.

"What are you doing here so late? Shouldn't you be home with your family?" Megan scolded playfully before closing the door behind him. "Are you hungry?"

"No, I've already eaten. Is grandfather around?" Damian smiled.

"He's in his office." Megan smiled before disappearing upstairs.

Damian found Tylen reading a letter of some sort which he quickly stuck it in a drawer then stood to move around the desk when Damian entered. Damian needed to talk so he sat down and began to explain to him everything that had happened tonight and told him the reason why Samuel had taken his marina. Surprisingly, Tylen never uttered a word or showed any emotion, he only told him to go home to his family as soon as he'd gotten what he'd needed. He then stood quietly and left him alone.

Tylen's unusual sullen and quiet mood piqued Damian's interest as to what he had been reading. Damian knew he should not have opened the drawer that was normally locked but his curiosity got the best of him. He convinced himself that he had his grandfather's best interest at heart so he pulled the old worn letter from the drawer and began reading. Damian's hands shook after reading the letter. He felt cold and numb. He placed the letter back into its resting place, gathered his file and left.

Damian's drive home was as if everything were in slow motion. He kept repeating the words in his head but no matter how hard he tried, he still could not believe what he'd just read: Samuel Blackheart was his biological father. His mother had slept with him out of anger and had gotten pregnant. Obviously, the letter never got mailed and he now understood why his grandfather and Carmen were having problems. He only wondered how his grandfather came about the letter. *How could mom keep this from me?* Damian wondered bitterly.

Damian and Madison were brother and sister, and Mallory could have been his daughter. Damian suddenly felt sick. He immediately pulled to the side of the road and threw up. It took him a minute to stop gagging and get himself together. He slowly drove home to his family.

Chapter Twenty-Nine

Angela knew what she was about to do would seal her fate forever but she didn't care anymore, so she convinced Lexie to meet her some place private and to come alone. Angela liked Lexie because she was real and you always knew where you stood with her, but she was also Tom-Tom's wife.

"I know you probably hate me and may be a little scared to be around me, but I promise I would never hurt you, as long as you stay completely honest with me," Angela told her.

"Okay, Angela, I can do that. Lexie stared hard at her. "I am so angry at you, but yet my heart goes out to you. I know there has to be something terribly wrong. I don't understand why you'd killed your sister and I know I never will, but it is not my place to judge. Only GOD has that privilege. You and Madison were the sisters I never had so I have to tell you that you need some serious help."

The way Lexie said that so seriously, especially that last part, was funny to Angela. She had to laugh. *I don't need any damn help. People just need to leave me the fuck alone.* "Anyways, I love you too, girl, but I need to let you know about Tom-Tom and me." For the first time since Angela had known Lexie she remained quite so Angela continued, "Remember back in the day after we all graduated?" Lexie remained quite as she nodded her head. "Well, after Tom-Tom and I dropped you off, we had sex. I've always thought you should know but I was afraid to tell because of Tom-Tom."

"Was that the only time?" She asked Angela.

Angela started to lie but Lexie was probably the

truest friend she'd ever had. "No." Angela stood to leave. "Right after you got pregnant a few months ago in your gazebo late one night, we did it but in his defense, he was drunk. Even the baby I aborted could have been his."

"Why are you telling me now? Is it because Tom-Tom has a hit out on you?" Lexie asked her calmly.

"Yes," Angela said and began to walk away then a thought occurred to her so she stopped. "If he tries to deny any of this tell him I told you about the mole on his inner left thigh."

I hope she leaves his ass. Hell, I would if a nigga had a bitch he fucked up in my house eating my food and playing with my kids. Overall Angela felt good because whatever happened would be worth it; she knew Lexie valued trust and honesty too much to just let this go. Angela could scratch Tom-Tom off her list because without Lexie or his kids, Tom-Tom was already dead.

***

Angela sat drinking her coffee and Kayla came to mind. She kind of felt sorry for her. Angela thought, *her stupid ass never should have opened the door for DeShun in the first place. Kayla knew DeShun had been pretty much strung out always trying to get her back and shit. No wonder DeShun took it from her; I heard her ass was even dressed like a tramp opening the door in nothing but a little red robe.*

At that moment, Angela felt overwhelmed. She thought of GOD and wished GOD could forgive her for all of the things she had done and the people she'd killed or caused to get killed, unfortunately she didn't think GOD would ever forgive a person like her. Angela immediately hardened her heart once again.

Angela thought back to when she was little girl. When she'd been twelve, Samuel raped her. He had said it was her fault for always running around in the woods wearing only a cut off T-shirt and short shorts. But she knew the real reason he started molesting her. He wanted her afraid because she caught her mother and him in bed together while her father had been working. Angela hadn't even planned on telling because her father had been always sneaking other women into the basement while her mother slept. Back in the day, Samuel and her father had been business partners for a while, that was until Samuel slithered in and cheated her father out of his share of the business.

Angela thought sadly about her mother and father. They died the night after her sixteenth birthday. It wasn't supposed to happen. It was meant for Samuel. Angela had been determined to get Samuel for everything he'd done. She'd put gas in his radiator, but she'd never expected her father's car to need repair and she sure didn't plan on him borrowing anything from Samuel.

Chapter Thirty

After arriving to work, Kayla became so sick she almost passed out. Ashland gave her her doctor's number. They scheduled Kayla in during her lunch break.

Kayla didn't have a lot of time, so the doctor ran a few blood tests and told her to take it easy and eat properly. Kayla told the nurse to just leave a message at home whenever her results returned. They all figured her iron might be low since she had been so busy she hadn't really had the time to eat properly. Kayla bought a sub sandwich and returned back to work; it was so busy that she didn't have time to think about anything other than work.

"Did you hear what Angela did?" Ashland asked her at the end of the day.

"No I hadn't. What did that crazy girl do this time?" Kayla joked as she organized some files.

Ashland stopped placing folders in a filing cabinet and looked at her seriously. "My mother called and told me Angela killed her sister."

Kayla couldn't respond so she just stood there as Ashland spoke. A chill rushed through her as she remembered her holding that gun to her temple. Ashland frowned and walked over to her. "You really hadn't heard anything?" Ashland questioned with a frown.

"No I hadn't, why?" Kayla looked at her questioningly.

"She stabbed DeShun last night also. He's in the hospital," Ashland said then added, "You ok?"

Kayla continued back to arranging the files. "I'm ok," she told her. Kayla didn't know what to think but she did feel bad for DeShun and even hoped he'd pull through alright.

Kayla's drive home was uneventful; she found Damian in the spare bedroom with shopping bags all over the floor. There were two different comforters lying on the floor – one with a princess pattern and the other with footballs. "What's this?" Kayla asked as she picked up one of the comforters off the floor. "Tymera and D'Neko are a little old for these."

"I know," Damian said uneasily then added, "Kayla, we need to talk. Come sit down," he told her. "I know a lot has happened, but I'm happy. I can't tell you how happy I am."

Kayla just sat and listened wondering what he was talking about.

"A nurse called today. You're pregnant," Damian said evenly.

Kayla sat quietly for a moment and wondered what happened to patient confidentiality, and then just as quickly it occurred to her that she had put Damian's name on a few consent forms. She wasn't mad though. She really didn't know what to say or how to respond to the news but what she did know was she loved Damian and would love to have his child. "I like the princess, but I'd be happy with the footballs," Kayla told Damian.

Damian looked at her in a way he couldn't interpret, but it made her feel good inside. "I love you, Kayla." He kissed her.

"Okay," Kayla said standing, "we're actually having a baby."

Damian stood and kissed her again. "I just wish my mom was here."

"And your dad," Kayla said.

"Yes and my dad," he added quietly then just as quickly smiled. "I don't want to wait anymore; pack your bags and let's go."

"Damian, I just can't up and leave; the kids have school and I have to work tomorrow."

"I called Jordan; they're going to stay with them for a couple of days. Ashland said it was ok for you to take off."

"Ok," Kayla smiled as she put her arms around his neck. "Where do you plan on taking me?"

"You know Jordan asked me what was the point of us waiting, when all we have to do is make our own memories of our wedding day. So, Miss Kayla, we are going away to get married, that is if you're ready."

"I'm ready," Kayla smiled as she threw a few pieces in an overnight bag.

Damian left the room. Kayla heard him telling the kids to pack a bag for a few days. Tymera was screaming excitedly about Damian officially becoming her father.

Chapter Thirty-One

After hearing that DeShun and Damian's test results showed they were not Mallory's father, Mo knew he had to step forward. Mo knew this would ruin his friendship with DeShun, but he didn't have a choice. He was thankful for Jarrod; even though Jarrod was upset with him, he still stood by him. Mo sat quietly as they listened intently to the doctor.

"She's in room 308 when you're ready to see her," the doctor said then was called away over the intercom.

A part of Mo was angry at Madison for not telling him the truth, but he took a calming breath because Madison was dead and Mallory needed him. Mo was her father. He stood to go visit his daughter.

Tom-Tom was in the room playing with Mallory; he stood as Mo entered. "What's up, Mo?" Tom-Tom said with a nod of his head.

"What up," Mo said with a returned nod.

Mallory sat up in bed and smiled as she held out her small hand. "Tom-Tom tells me you're my real daddy."

Mo was somewhat taken aback by her maturity. For someone so small she sounded very grown up and smart, just like he imagined her mom did when she was her age. Mo couldn't help but smile as he took her tiny hand in his.

Tom-Tom stood. "Well I'm going to visit Jarrod out in the hallway while you talk to your dad a few minutes, then I'll be back." He kissed her on top of her head as he left the room.

Mallory was very charming for her age and before

they knew it, Tom-Tom was back in the room followed by a nurse, who checked her vitals.

"As soon as the doctor is available he'll be releasing her." The nurse smiled at Mo before leaving the room.

Mo panicked because he had no idea how to take care of a little girl.

Mallory looked up at Mo. "Would it be ok if I stayed with Tom-Tom tonight?"

"Sure, that will give me a chance to get a room fixed up for you," Mo said to her.

Her smile faltered as she asked them slowly, "Is my daddy, I mean, *DeShun*, going to be ok?"

"Yes he is, honey," Tom-Tom answered as he kissed her.

Mallory looked at Mo curiously. "Are you married or do you have anymore kids? I hope so because I really hate being an only child."

Tom-Tom and Mo laughed at the same time. "I'm not married and you're my only child," Mo said to her.

"That you know about, huh?" She laughed innocently when she said that. "You never thought you'd have me, did you?" She said staring up at Mo.

"No, I didn't, but I have you now and maybe in a few years you'll get a brother or sister.

That is, after I find me a wife," Mo said to her. He once again wondered how DeShun would react to the news of Mallory being his daughter.

The doctor entered the room and after giving instructions and signing release papers, Mo watched as Mallory left with Tom-Tom. DeShun was finally in stable condition.

Chapter Thirty-Two

After Tom-Tom arrived home, Mallory noticed the kids playing in the yard so decided to join Alyssa, his nine-year-old, who was sitting in the grass reading. He was proud of Mallory's strength and determination and couldn't help but smile as she hobbled on her crutches to join her. He wasn't quite sure about Mo taking care of her, but maybe this was what he needed to slow down his partying. Tom-Tom was just glad DeShun wasn't her father but he still planned on keeping a close eye on Mallory just to make sure Mo did what he was supposed to.

As Tom-Tom looked around he was happy where his life was. He had a beautiful wife who had given him six wonderful kids and one on the way. He smiled to himself as went to find his wife, who was in the kitchen.

"I'm back," Tom-Tom said walking up behind her kissing her softly on her neck and rubbing her belly. "The lasagna smells delicious." Lexie really didn't say anything; she continued to prepare the garlic bread. "You ok?" Tom-Tom asked her.

Lexie moved away from him to place the bread in the oven. "I'm fine." She never looked at him as she spoke.

Tom-Tom sat down and studied his wife. He knew something was wrong but had no idea what. He wondered if maybe it was the baby bothering her. He was about to press the issue but Malik, their oldest, entered the kitchen so he made himself a mental note to find out later. As usual, he helped Lexie prepared the plates for the kids and they all sat down to a nice dinner.

After cleaning the kitchen and taking a hot shower, Tom-Tom sat on the edge of the bed with his towel still wrapped around his waist and waited on Lexie to come to bed. He laid back and closed his eyes for a few minutes and thought about everything that had taken place. He still couldn't believe Madison was gone and it was truly surprising to learn Mo was Mallory's father. At least now DeShun will finally know the true meaning of betrayal.

Angela came to mind; Tom-Tom truly regretted the things that had taken place between them. After graduation he allowed himself to become seduced by her and again only just a few short months ago. Lexie had just found out she was pregnant again and was understandably upset. She hadn't felt like having sex and one night after being sexless for almost two months, he got drunk and once again allowed himself to be seduced by Angela. Thank goodness she aborted that baby, because he wasn't even sure if it wasn't his. He sat up because he didn't feel like thinking about Angela anymore and wondered what was taking Lexie so long. He had a gut feeling and he didn't like it, because those feelings were usually on point. He found a pair of jeans and a t-shirt and decided to find out what was up with his wife.

Tom-Tom looked through the house and decided to check the yard and couldn't find Lexie. He was walking back toward the house when he saw a light on from a third floor bedroom. He frowned because they only used that area for guests.

Tom-Tom found Lexie sitting up in bed reading her bible. "Lexie, what's going on? Why are here?" He asked but didn't think he really wanted to hear her answer.

Lexie closed her bible and got out of bed to close the bedroom door. "Let's sit." She led him to an adjacent room made for reading and TV. "I met with Angela today."

He immediately tensed when he heard Angela's name. He couldn't say a word he only listened to see what Angela had told her.

"She told me you had sex with her after graduation. Is that true?" She asked.

"Yes," Tom-Tom responded honestly without trying to think of a lie. That had occurred so long ago hopefully she would forgive him. Maybe if he had told her about the first time, she would have never wanted to have Angela around so much. Maybe even the second time never would have happened. But as he looked into Lexie's eyes he immediately regretted giving into his lust and especially regretted not denying it.

Lexie took a deep breath. "What about down in the gazebo?"

Now it was Tom-Tom's turn to take a deep breath; he could only nod his head. He felt less than a man for hurting her, and even lower for doing it with his very own cousin. He couldn't respond, but before he could blink Lexie had stood and began swinging on him. For someone so small and pregnant, she was awfully strong. It took all he had to hold her still. "Lexie, stop! The baby, you're going to hurt the baby!" She kicked him again missing his groin only by inches. She punched him in his eye. "Damn it, Lexie, I said stop!" Tom-Tom had to maneuver his body as to not hurt the baby. They were both breathing heavily.

"Let me go," she said surprisingly calmly.

Hesitantly he did as asked. Cautiously he stood to sit across from her.

Lexie spoke calmly, precisely and without emotion. "From this point on, the third floor is off limits to you and we are married by name only. I expect you to take care of me and your children as usual because I will not be leaving this house. I've worked too hard taking care of you and the kids to give up my home. You can stay or go, that choice is yours, but you will not ever be sharing my bed again."

Tom-Tom was in shock, he couldn't even move. He looked over at Lexie and all he saw was disgust in her eyes.

Lexie stood to look out the window and said softly, "You could have at least tried to deny the last time. I would have believed you even though she told me about your mole. Please leave me alone."

Tom-Tom wanted so badly to go over and hold her but he knew that's not what she wanted or needed. His eyes were burning, but not from where she had punched him, but because he knew she would not forgive him. This would take some time. After a minute he stood and left her alone.

In his bedroom, Tom-Tom sat for the longest debating on what to do. Angela came to mind and the pain over what he'd done to Lexie had instantly turned to hatred. He reached for his cell and called the one person he trusted to come through the fastest. "Hey, I need you to find Angela as quickly as possible, and when you do, stay put and call me." He closed his cell wanting to throw it across the room but he didn't. He needed it because it would tell him where Angela was. "That bitch is dead."

Chapter Thirty-Three

After leaving the hospital, DeShun was very sore and thankful for the pain pills. That morning he had awakened only to find a cop standing over him. That had scared the hell out of him, but he had only been there to ask a few questions about Angela. He had a feeling his luck was running out so he was glad when Mo came in and checked him out of that hospital. Mo even asked him to stay with him until he fully recuperated. DeShun smiled, *that's my boy, always did have my back.* They left the hospital.

"How's Mallory doing?" DeShun asked Mo.

"She's good, but I do need to talk to you about her," Mo said sitting down across from him.

DeShun sat back and relaxed, glad to be out that hospital. "Sure, what's up? She's alright isn't she? Is she still with Tom-Tom?"

"Yeah, she's still at Tom-Tom's and she's doing fine." Mo stood and walked back and forth.

"Come on now sit down. All that walking is driving me crazy," DeShun joked.

"My bad." Mo sat down. "Listen, there is something you need to know. I really don't know how to say it, so I'm gonna come out with it." Mo took a deep breath. "Mallory isn't your daughter. She's mine."

I don't believe this shit. My boy, my best friend and my cousin turned out to be my daughter's father. No wonder he and Madison used to get along so well. Damn Angela for stabbing me. DeShun stood slowly. "You know you best be glad Angela hooked me real good." DeShun turned around and slowly picked up his bag. "I'm out."

Mo just watched as DeShun walked out his front

door and out of his life for good.

When DeShun got home he was tired and angry as he thought to himself, *damn, I hadn't realized how bad it would hurt to find out a child wasn't yours. Shit, if Kayla ever told me anything like that about Tymera or D'Neko I know I wouldn't be held accountable for what I'd do to her. D'Neko couldn't stand me but he was mine. His ass is just like me when I was his age. I couldn't stand my own damn daddy either.*

DeShun had to sit down because when he thought everything over, he really had no one. *Here I am just getting home from the hospital and I'm completely alone.* He couldn't help but laugh. His phone rang and it was someone letting him know that he didn't get the job because of the pending rape charge against him. DeShun knew Damian was behind it. Mo had told him Damian had had put the word out that he was a rapist and he'd be lucky to get a job at a fast food joint. DeShun leaned back in the rocking chair and closed his eyes to take a short nap. Next thing he knew, someone kicked him awake and he was tied to the chair.

"Wake your ass up," Angela said as she sat on an end table in front of DeShun with her legs spread wide and her hair looking wild and uncontrollable as she ate a piece of dried toast. The jeans that she wore were tight; he tried to look away but he could not deny his attraction for her. DeShun laughed as he thought a*s crazy as it all sounds, my stupid ass was tied to a chair by a crazed lunatic of a woman, and here I am having a damn hard on.* He wanted to be angry at her, he should be angry but he only felt sorry for her.

"What? You come back to finish the job?" DeShun said laughing even though he was scared.

"Not yet. Tell me what's going on. Have you heard anything about me or Tom-Tom?" Angela asked carelessly.

He laughed again. "When he finds you, you're

finished."

She stood quietly as she washed her hands.

"Angela, why are you here if you don't plan on killing me? I don't want to get caught up with you and Tom-Tom," DeShun told her honestly.

She laughed. "I needed some news. I figured Mo had told you something."

"He did. He told me how you fucked up Tom-Tom's marriage," he said boldly.

Angela remained speechless.

"Come on and untie me," he said to her.

"Why couldn't you just love me? Was Madison that perfect?" She suddenly asked him quietly from across the room.

DeShun didn't know what to say and he damn sure didn't want to set her off, but to be honest, Angela was just the kind of woman men only wanted to have sex with, a woman that would do any and everything at any time and any place. "Madison and I have been through a lot together, but she wasn't what she appeared to be. Mallory turned out not to be mine, your sister was sleeping around with Mo. He's actually Mallory's father. You can put your mind at ease because Madison was far from perfect."

Angela walked up quietly and untied him. She grabbed her bag then left without another word.

DeShun sat for the longest thinking over things and came to the conclusion that there was nothing left for him here and he needed to get the hell out of town too. Maybe his kids, but they're really not his because he never really did anything for them; he only donated his sperm to Kayla. He decided to pack his few belongings and leave.

***

As DeShun was heading out of town he saw D'Neko and a group of his friends hanging out at the park. "D'Neko!" he yelled as he walked toward the fence.

■■

D'Neko silently stood before him. He could tell he wasn't too thrilled to see him.

"I just wanted to see you and Tymera before I left," he told D'Neko but the look he was giving him told him he could care less.

"Tymera don't need you popping in and out of her life anymore. She's happy right now, Damian is good to her and he ain't gon' leave us the way you always do. Why you always have to get her all upset? You always telling us you'll be there and never show up, even when you promise. Tymera always end up crying. You ain't my daddy. I ain't got a damn daddy. Why don't you just leave us the fuck alone?" D'Neko said looking DeShun straight in his eyes.

"Boy, you best recognize who you talking to." DeShun wanted to jack his ass up but he heard the truth in his words.

D'Neko bravely and boldly stared harder at his father, letting all of his hatred and animosity show. "I know who I'm talking to. You the man that likes to beat on my moms." D'Neko had the nerve to get up in his face. "You that bitch-ass nigga that raped my moms, you also that motherfucker that almost killed my momma. Maybe Angela should have finished what she started and killed your sorry ass."

Something inside of DeShun snapped and he grabbed D'Neko and shoved him hard up against the fence. He ignored the twinge of pain in his stomach. "Boy, you best watch who the fuck you talk to like that."

"What you gon'do? Beat me too? I ain't scared of you anymore," D'Neko said as his eyes glistened angrily.

DeShun instantly stepped back. He knew D'Neko was lost to him. He was only twelve years old but he seemed so much older. DeShun just turned around and walked away. He could only pray that maybe one day things would be better between them.

Chapter Thirty-Four

He had been following Angela almost all night and she finally settled in at a Hilton Inn. He pulled out the card she'd given him and decided to give her a call. "Angela, I'm not sure if you remember me but we met about two weeks ago at the medical convention."

Angela was being very cautious. She would not meet him where she was staying; instead they met at a restaurant twenty minutes away. By looking at her she seemed calm, as if she didn't have a care in the world. They sat at the bar and he ordered two rum and cokes.

"I don't even know your name," Angela sipped her mixed drink.

He smiled at her directness. "Bobby"

"Just Bobby, no last name?" She inquired lightly with a raised eyebrow.

He laughed. "Yes, I do have a last name. Let's begin again." He held out his hand for her to shake. "Hi. I'm Bobby Kidderman." He didn't give out his name too often, but decided to in this case. "And I find you to be very exquisite." He smiled as he lied. Angela was an attractive girl but she was far from exquisite.

Angela took his hand and laughed mockingly. "It's very nice to meet you Mr. Kidderman."

He smiled as he eased his hand away. "What's so funny?"

"You could have thought of something better than Kidderman," she told him and it was his turn to laugh.

"Believe it or not, that's actually my last name. You wouldn't believe half the jokes I receive because of it," he told her. Angela seemed to relax instantly.

"Ok, Bobby Kidderman, I'm hungry - do you plan on feeding me?"

He got them a table and they placed their order.

After dinner he suggested they take a walk outside.

"Would you like to come back to my room?" Angela asked.

He laughed inside because there was no way in hell he'd ever touch her, even if he had on three rubbers. "Okay, but I have someplace better in mind," he told her seductively as he smiled.

Angela smiled and excused herself to the ladies' room. His cell vibrated. He ignored Tom-Tom's call. They had Angela right where they wanted her.

As he drove, Angela remained quiet. It was a pleasant drive. The scenery to the mountains was beautiful. He knew what he had to do and he'd do it. He wouldn't think about it. Thinking too much could sometimes cost you.

"Here we are." He smiled as he stretched. It had taken almost an hour to get there. He knew Tom-Tom was somewhere close by and would let his presence be known when the time was right.

"Wow. Is this your place?" Angela smiled and seemed so innocent at the moment, he almost felt sorry for her. He removed his keys to unlock his front door. This was his haven. Rarely did he allow anyone there. Unfortunately Angela wouldn't be there long.

"Bobby Kidderman, this place is amazing. You live here all alone?" She asked.

"I wouldn't call it all alone. There are the usual bears, mountain lions, bob cats and so forth." Tom-Tom sat smiling waiting like the predator he was.

Angela laughed contemptuously. "Tom-Tom, how are Lexie and the kids?"

Tom-Tom ignored her question and continued to smile. "You know, not too many people know my friend's real name. Unless of course you grew up or went to college with him. Those unfortunate ones that he tells while he's working, well let's just say that's their kiss of death." Tom-Tom stood. "Too bad he didn't give you an alias. Oh well." Tom-Tom turned his back to Angela to stare out the window.

Angela noticed for the first time she and Tom-Tom were alone. Bobby had seemed to vanish. Angela became nervous. "Tom-Tom, look I'm sorry. I didn't mean to tell Lexie about us. I was just mad at you. I'll tell her I was lying and straighten everything out for you."

Tom-Tom laughed. "It's too late." Tom-Tom faced Angela and leaned against the windowpane. "You are a real piece of work. I'll admit you give amazing head, other than that you're filth, trash, straight garbage, nothing but a straight up trick-ass ho. You weren't even that good of a fuck for me to lose Lexie over."

For the first time Angela noticed plastic covered the floor and furniture where she stood. She immediately moved towards the doorway. It was closed and locked.

Tom-Tom once again turned his back to Angela. "Can't get out, Bobby locked us in. It's just you and me, so I would advise you to pull out all of your little toys right now. Your best bet is to kill me while you have a chance because I'm going to kill you." Tom-Tom casually turned around to face Angela once again. He leaned casually back as he watched Angela fumble with her purse only to drop it. Tom-Tom laughed. "Damn, Angela, I hadn't realized you were the nervous sort. You always seem so cool and controlled."

"Tom-Tom, blood is blood. You can't do this!" Angela cried.

Tom-Tom walked casually over to Angela and grabbed her chin and whispered, "Just like Madison." He shot Angela repeatedly. A bullet for each person she'd killed. He stepped back and cursed.

Bobby stood in the doorway. "What's the matter, had a change of heart?" He asked as he looked at Angela's slumped form lying on the floor.

"Hell no, I just bought this damn shirt. I was in such a hurry to get here I forgot to change."

"Taken care of, your replacements are upstairs pressed and ironed. Go home to your family, I'll handle the rest." He watched Tom-Tom walk away but he knew he really didn't have a real family to go home to. Tom-Tom only had his kids. It would be a long time before Lexie would be his wife again. Bobby began the process of clearing away Angela's existence.

***

After cleaning and discarding away all evidence of what had occurred, it was late and Bobby was restless. He needed a new job quick. He stood to pour himself a drink. His cell vibrated. Tom-Tom was calling. "What up?" He asked.

"I have another daughter. She was born while I was handling my business today at your place," Tom-Tom said but he sounded off. Bobby figured everything was beginning to get to him.

"Hey, that's good. Congrats, man. How's Lexie doing?" Bobby asked.

"She died in child birth," Tom-Tom said softly and cleared his throat. "Listen, just wanted you to hear it from me. I have to see about my kids. I'll holla at you later." Tom-Tom disconnected the call.

Bobby killed his drink and fixed another. While Tom-Tom had been here killing Angela, Lexie was dying while giving birth to his daughter. "Life is a fucking bitch,"

Bobby said out loud to no one in particular. No sooner did he speak those words than a chill suddenly sweep over him. *Enter by the narrow gate; for wide is the gate and broad is the way that leads to destruction, and there are many who go in by it. Because narrow is the gate and difficult is the way which leads to life, and there are few who find it.* Bobby stood thinking of his father. He tried shaking off that strange feeling as he finished the remainder of his drink. He forced himself to think of Damian's parents. At least now that Angela is gone, Carmen and Mitchell would soon be out of hiding. Luckily for them they had been staying in one of the other cottages until a few repairs could be made on the one they'd purchased.

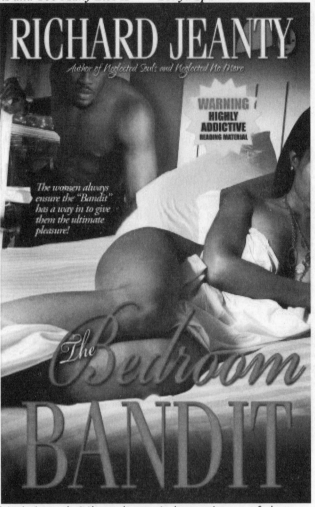

It may not be Histeria Lane, but these desperate housewives are fed up with their neglecting husbands. Their sexual needs take precedence over the millions of dollars their husbands bring home every year to keep them happy in their affluent neighborhood. While their husbands claim to be hard at work, these wives are doing a little work of their own with the bedroom bandit. Is the bandit swift enough to evade these angry husbands?

In Stores!!

NEGLECTED SOULS

Motherhood and the trials of loving too hard and not enough frame this story...The realism of these characters will bring tears to your spirit as you discover the hero in the villain you never saw coming...

In Stores!!!

Jimmy and Nina continue to feel a void in their lives
because they haven't a clue about their genealogical makeup. Jimmy falls victims to a life threatening illness and only
the right organ donor can save his life. Will the donor be the
bridge to reconnect Jimmy and Nina to their biological
family? Will Nina be the strength for her brother in his time
of need? Will they ever find out what really happened to
their mother?

In Stores!!!

Betrayal, lust, lies, murder, deception, sex and tainted love frame this story... Julian Stevens lacks the ambition and freak ability that Miko looks for in a man, but she married him despite his flaws to spite an ex-boyfriend. When Miko least expects it, the old boyfriend shows up and ready to sweep her off her feet again. She wants to have her cake and eat it too. While Miko's doing her own thing, Julian is determined to become everything Miko ever wanted in a man and more, but will he go to extreme lengths to prove he's worthy of Miko's love? Julian Stevens soon finds out that he's capable of being more than he could ever imagine as he embarks on a journey that will change his life forever.

In Stores!!!

The police in New York and other major cities around the country are increasingly victimizing black men. The violence has escalated to deadly force, most of the time without justification. In this controversial book, noted author Richard Jeanty, tackles the problem of police brutality and the unfair treatment of Black men at the hands of police in New York City and the rest of the country.

In Stores!!!

Just when Darren thinks his relationship with Tina is flourishing, there is yet another hurdle on the road hindering their bliss. Tina saw a therapist for months to deal with her sexual addiction, but now Darren is wondering if she was ever treated completely. Darren has not been taking care of home and Tina's frustrated and agrees to a break-up with Darren. Will Darren lose Tina for good? Will Tina ever realize that Darren is the best man for her?

In Stores!!

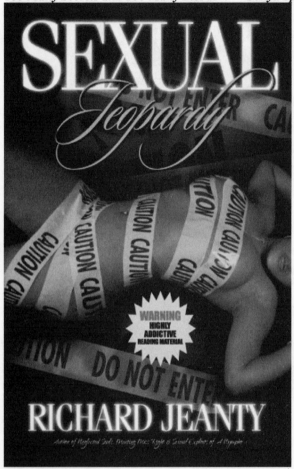

Ronald Murphy was a player all his life until he and his best friend, Myles, met the women of their dreams during a brief vacation in South Beach, Florida. Sexual Jeopardy is story of trust, betrayal, forgiveness, friendship and hope.

In Stores!!!

Tina develops an insatiable sexual appetite very early in life. She
only loves her boyfriend, Darren, but he's too far away in college to satisfy her sexual needs.
Tina decides to get buck wild away in college
Will her sexual trysts jeopardize the lives of the men in her life?

In Stores!!!

Faith Jones, a woman in her mid-thirties, has given up on ever finding love again until she met her son's best friend, Darius. Faith Jones is walking a thin line of betrayal against her son for the love of Darius. Will Faith allow her emotions to outweigh her common sense?

In Stores!!!

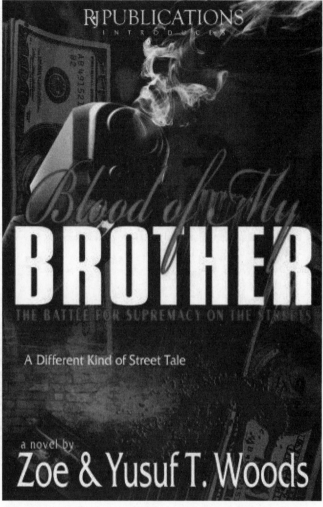

Roc was the man on the streets of Philadelphia, until his younger brother decided it was time to become his own man by wreaking havoc on Roc's crew without any regards for the blood relation they share. Drug, murder, mayhem and the pursuit of happiness can lead to deadly consequences. This story can only be told by a person who has lived it.

In Stores!!!

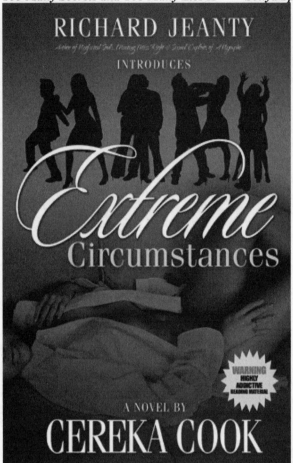

What happens when a devoted woman is betrayed? Come take a ride with Chanel as she takes her boyfriend, Donnell, to circumstances beyond belief after he betrays her trust with his endless infidelities. How long can Chanel's friend, Janai, use her looks to get what she wants from men before it catches up to her? Find out as Janai's gold-digging ways catch up with and she has to face the consequences of her extreme actions.

In Stores!!!

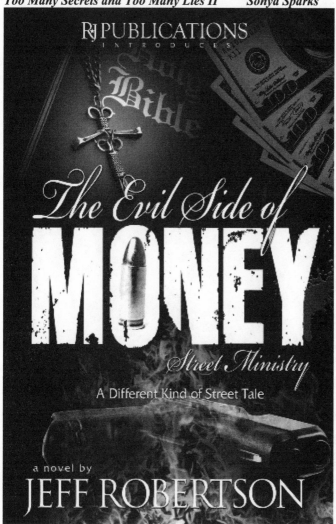

Violence, Intimidation and carnage are the order as Nathan and his brother set out to build the most powerful drug empires in Chicago. However, when God comes knocking, Nathan's conscience starts to surface. Will his haunted criminal past get the best of him?

In Stores!!

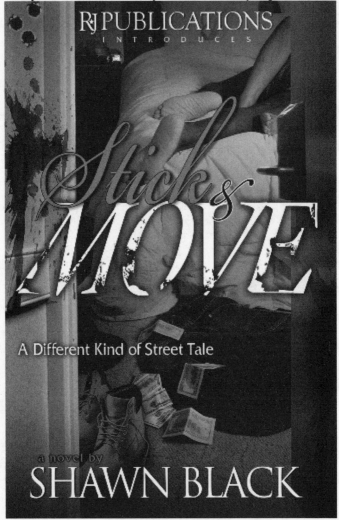

RJ PUBLICATIONS
INTRODUCES

Stick &
MOVE

A Different Kind of Street Tale

a novel by
SHAWN BLACK

Yasmina witnessed the brutal murder of her parents at a young age at the hand of a drug dealer. This event stained her mind and upbringing as a result. Will Yamina's life come full circle with her past? Find out as Yasmina's crew, The Platinum Chicks, set out to make a name for themselves on the street.

In stores!!

Ashland's mother, Bianca, fights hard to suppress the truth from her daughter because she doesn't want her to marry Jordan, the grandson of an ex-lover she loathes. Ashland soon finds out how cruel and vengeful her mother can be, but what price will Bianca pay for redemption?

In stores!!

Malcolm is a wealthy virgin who decides to conceal his wealth
From the world until he meets the right woman. His wealthy best
friend, Dexter, hides his wealth from no one. Malcolm struggles to
find love in an environment where vanity and materialism are
rampant, while Dexter is getting more than enough of his share of
women. Malcolm needs develop self-esteem and confidence to
meet the right woman and Dexter's confidence is borderline
arrogance.
Will bad boys like Dexter continue to take women for a ride?

Or will nice guys like Malcolm continue to finish last?

In Stores!!!

What happens when a woman's devotion to her fiancee is tested weeks before she gets married? What if her fiancee is just hiding behind the veil of ministry to deceive her? Find out as Sean Mitchell takes you on a journey you'll never forget into the lives of Angelica, Titus and Aurelius.

In Stores!!

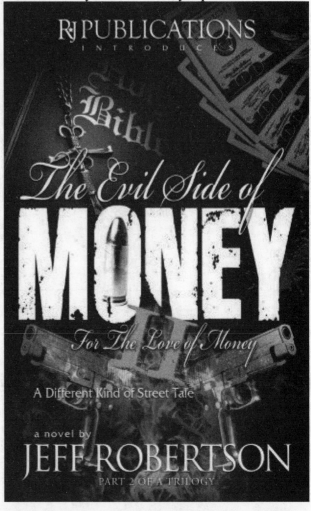

A beautigul woman from Bolivia threatens the existence of the drug empire that Nate and G have built. While Nate is head over heels for her, G can see right through her. As she brings on more conflict between the crew, G sets out to show Nate exactly who she is before she brings about their demise.

In Stores!!!

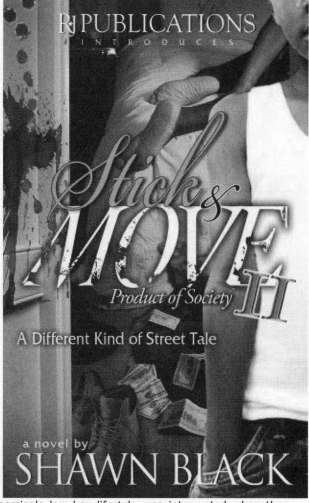

Scorcher and Yasmina's low key lifestyle was interrupted when they were taken down by the Feds, but their daughter, Serosa, was left to be raised by the foster care system. Will Serosa become a product of her environment or will she rise above it all? Her bloodline is undeniable, but will she be able to control it?

In Stores!!

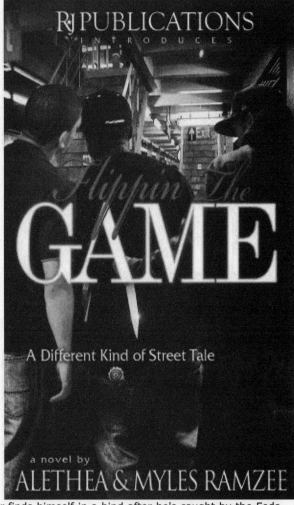

An ex-drug dealer finds himself in a bind after he's caught by the Feds. He has to decide which is more important, his family or his loyalty to the game. As he fights hard to make a decision, those who helped him to the top fear the worse from him. Will he get the chance to tell the govt. whole story, or will someone get to him before he becomes a snitch?

In Stores!!!

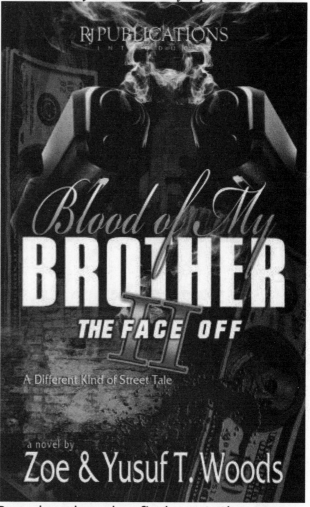

What will Roc do when he finds out the true identity of Solo? Will the blood shed come from his own brother Lil Mac? Will Roc and Solo take their beef to an explosive height on the street? Find out as Zoe and Yusuf bring the second installment to their hot street joint, Blood of My Brother.

In Stores!!!

Dave Richardson is enjoying success as his second book became a New York Times best-seller. He left the life of The Bedroom behind to settle with his family, but an obsessed fan has not had enough of Dave and she will go to great length to get a piece of him. How far will a woman go to get a man that doesn't belong to her?

Coming September 2010

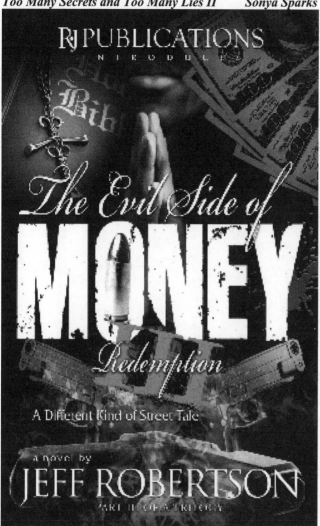

Forced to abandon the drug world for good, Nathan and G attempt to change their lives and move forward, but will their past come back to haunt them? This final installment will leave you speechless.

Coming November 2009

Nafys Muhammad managed to beat the charges in court, but will he beat them on the street? There will be many revelations in this story as betrayal, greed, sex scandal corruption and murder unravels throughout every page. Get ready for a rough ride.

Coming December 2009

Deon is at the mercy of a ruthless gang that kidnapped him. In a foreign land where he knows nothing about the culture, he has to use his survival instincts and his wit to outsmart his captors. Will the Hoodfellas show up in time to rescue Deon, or will Crazy D take over once again and fight an all out war by himself?

Coming March 2010

While Yasmina sits on death row awaiting her fate, her daughter, Serosa, is fighting the fight of her life on the outside. Her genetic structure that indirectly bins her to her parents could also be her downfall and force her to see that there's no way out!

Coming January 2010

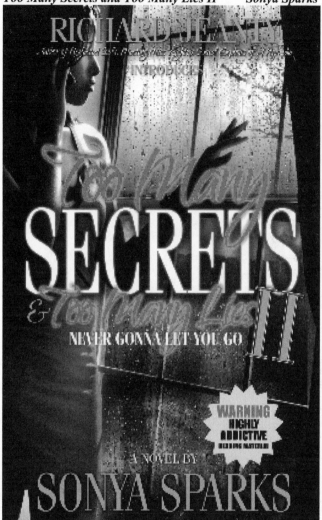

The drama continues as Deshun is hunted by Angela who still feels that ex-girlfriend Kayla is still trying to win his heart, though he brutally raped her. Angela will kill anyone who gets in her way, but is DeShun worth all the aggravation?

Coming September 2009

Buck Johnson was forced to make the best out of worst situation. He has witnessed the most cruel events in his life and it is those events who the man that he has become. Was the Johnson family ignorant souls through no fault of their own?

Coming October 2009

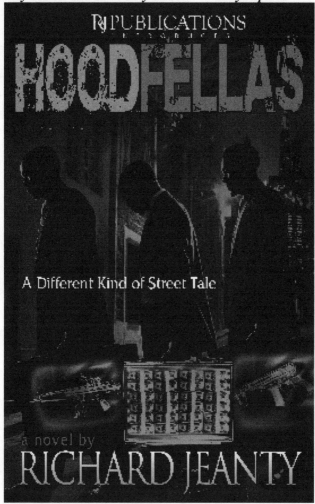

When an Ex-con finds himself destitute and in dire need of the basic necessities after he's released from prison, he turns to what he knows best, crime, but at what cost? Extortion, murder and mayhem drives him back to the top, but will he stay there?

In Stores !!!

What happens when someone falls insanely in love?
Stalking is just the beginning.
In Stores!!!

Use this coupon to order by mail
1. Neglected Souls, Richard Jeanty $14.95
2. Neglected No More, Richard Jeanty $14.95
3. Ignorant Souls, Richard Jeanty $15.00, October 2009
4. Sexual Exploits of Nympho, Richard Jeanty $14.95
5. Meeting Ms. Right's Whip Appeal, Richard Jeanty $14.95
6. Me and Mrs. Jones, K.M Thompson $14.95
7. Chasin' Satisfaction, W.S Burkett $14.95
8. Extreme Circumstances, Cereka Cook $14.95
9. The Most Dangerous Gang In America, R. Jeanty $15.00
10. Sexual Exploits of a Nympho II, Richard Jeanty $15.00
11. Sexual Jeopardy, Richard Jeanty $14.95
12. Too Many Secrets, Too Many Lies, Sonya Sparks $15.00
13. Stick And Move, Shawn Black $15.00 Available
14. Evil Side Of Money, Jeff Robertson $15.00
15. Evil Side Of Money II, Jeff Robertson $15.00
16. Evil Side Of Money III, Jeff Robertson $15.00
17. Flippin' The Game, Alethea and M. Ramzee, $15.00 Available
18. Flippin' The Game II, Alethea and M. Ramzee, $15.00 Dec. 2009
19. Cater To Her, W.S Burkett $15.00
20. Blood of My Brother I, Zoe & Yusuf Woods $15.00
21. Blood of my Brother II, Zoe & Ysuf Woods $15.00
22. Hoodfellas, Richard Jeanty $15.00 available
23. Hoodfellas II, Richard Jeanty, $15.00 03/30/2010
24. The Bedroom Bandit, Richard Jeanty $15.00 Available
25. Mr. Erotica, Richard Jeanty, $15.00, Sept 2010
26. Stick N Move II, Shawn Black $15.00 Available
27. Stick N Move III, Shawn Black $15.00 Jan, 2010
28. Miami Noire, W.S. Burkett $15.00 Available
29. Insanely In Love, Cereka Cook $15.00 Available
30. Blood of My Brother III, Zoe & Yusuf Woods September 2009

Name_____

Address_____

City_____State_____Zip Code_____

Please send the novels that I have circled above.
Shipping and Handling: Free
Total Number of Books_____
Total Amount Due_____
        Buy 3 books and get 1 free. This offer is subject to change without notice.
Send institution check or money order (no cash or CODs) to:
RJ Publications
PO Box 300771
Jamaica, NY 11434
For more information please call 718-471-2926, or visit www.rjpublications.com

Please allow 2-3 weeks for delivery.

Use this coupon to order by mail
31. Neglected Souls, Richard Jeanty $14.95
32. Neglected No More, Richard Jeanty $14.95
33. Ignorant Souls, Richard Jeanty $15.00, October 2009
34. Sexual Exploits of Nympho, Richard Jeanty $14.95
35. Meeting Ms. Right's Whip Appeal, Richard Jeanty $14.95
36. Me and Mrs. Jones, K.M Thompson $14.95
37. Chasin' Satisfaction, W.S Burkett $14.95
38. Extreme Circumstances, Cereka Cook $14.95
39. The Most Dangerous Gang In America, R. Jeanty $15.00
40. Sexual Exploits of a Nympho II, Richard Jeanty $15.00
41. Sexual Jeopardy, Richard Jeanty $14.95
42. Too Many Secrets, Too Many Lies, Sonya Sparks $15.00
43. Stick And Move, Shawn Black $15.00 Available
44. Evil Side Of Money, Jeff Robertson $15.00
45. Evil Side Of Money II, Jeff Robertson $15.00
46. Evil Side Of Money III, Jeff Robertson $15.00
47. Flippin' The Game, Alethea and M. Ramzee, $15.00 Available
48. Flippin' The Game II, Alethea and M. Ramzee, $15.00 Dec. 2009
49. Cater To Her, W.S Burkett $15.00
50. Blood of My Brother I, Zoe & Yusuf Woods $15.00
51. Blood of my Brother II, Zoe & Ysuf Woods $15.00
52. Hoodfellas, Richard Jeanty $15.00 available
53. Hoodfellas II, Richard Jeanty, $15.00 03/30/2010
54. The Bedroom Bandit, Richard Jeanty $15.00 Available
55. Mr. Erotica, Richard Jeanty, $15.00, Sept 2010
56. Stick N Move II, Shawn Black $15.00 Available
57. Stick N Move III, Shawn Black $15.00 Jan, 2010
58. Miami Noire, W.S. Burkett $15.00 Available
59. Insanely In Love, Cereka Cook $15.00 Available
60. Blood of My Brother III, Zoe & Yusuf Woods September 2009

Name_____
Address_____
City_____State_____Zip Code_____

Please send the novels that I have circled above.
Shipping and Handling: Free
Total Number of Books_____
Total Amount Due_____
     Buy 3 books and get 1 free. This offer is subject to change without notice.
Send institution check or money order (no cash or CODs) to:
RJ Publications
PO Box 300771
Jamaica, NY 11434
For more information please call 718-471-2926, or visit www.rjpublications.com

Please allow 2-3 weeks for delivery.

Use this coupon to order by mail

61. Neglected Souls, Richard Jeanty $14.95
62. Neglected No More, Richard Jeanty $14.95
63. Ignorant Souls, Richard Jeanty $15.00, October 2009
64. Sexual Exploits of Nympho, Richard Jeanty $14.95
65. Meeting Ms. Right's Whip Appeal, Richard Jeanty $14.95
66. Me and Mrs. Jones, K.M Thompson $14.95
67. Chasin' Satisfaction, W.S Burkett $14.95
68. Extreme Circumstances, Cereka Cook $14.95
69. The Most Dangerous Gang In America, R. Jeanty $15.00
70. Sexual Exploits of a Nympho II, Richard Jeanty $15.00
71. Sexual Jeopardy, Richard Jeanty $14.95
72. Too Many Secrets, Too Many Lies, Sonya Sparks $15.00
73. Stick And Move, Shawn Black $15.00 Available
74. Evil Side Of Money, Jeff Robertson $15.00
75. Evil Side Of Money II, Jeff Robertson $15.00
76. Evil Side Of Money III, Jeff Robertson $15.00
77. Flippin' The Game, Alethea and M. Ramzee, $15.00 Available
78. Flippin' The Game II, Alethea and M. Ramzee, $15.00 Dec. 2009
79. Cater To Her, W.S Burkett $15.00
80. Blood of My Brother I, Zoe & Yusuf Woods $15.00
81. Blood of my Brother II, Zoe & Ysuf Woods $15.00
82. Hoodfellas, Richard Jeanty $15.00 available
83. Hoodfellas II, Richard Jeanty, $15.00 03/30/2010
84. The Bedroom Bandit, Richard Jeanty $15.00 Available
85. Mr. Erotica, Richard Jeanty, $15.00, Sept 2010
86. Stick N Move II, Shawn Black $15.00 Available
87. Stick N Move III, Shawn Black $15.00 Jan, 2010
88. Miami Noire, W.S. Burkett $15.00 Available
89. Insanely In Love, Cereka Cook $15.00 Available
90. Blood of My Brother III, Zoe & Yusuf Woods September 2009

Name_____

Address_____

City_____State_____Zip Code_____

Please send the novels that I have circled above.
Shipping and Handling: Free
Total Number of Books_____
Total Amount Due_____
Buy 3 books and get 1 free. This offer is subject to change without notice.
Send institution check or money order (no cash or CODs) to:
RJ Publications
PO Box 300771
Jamaica, NY 11434
For more information please call 718-471-2926, or visit www.rjpublications.com

Please allow 2-3 weeks for delivery.

Use this coupon to order by mail
91. Neglected Souls, Richard Jeanty $14.95
92. Neglected No More, Richard Jeanty $14.95
93. Ignorant Souls, Richard Jeanty $15.00, October 2009
94. Sexual Exploits of Nympho, Richard Jeanty $14.95
95. Meeting Ms. Right's Whip Appeal, Richard Jeanty $14.95
96. Me and Mrs. Jones, K.M Thompson $14.95
97. Chasin' Satisfaction, W.S Burkett $14.95
98. Extreme Circumstances, Cereka Cook $14.95
99. The Most Dangerous Gang In America, R. Jeanty $15.00
100. Sexual Exploits of a Nympho II, Richard Jeanty $15.00
101. Sexual Jeopardy, Richard Jeanty $14.95
102. Too Many Secrets, Too Many Lies, Sonya Sparks $15.00
103. Stick And Move, Shawn Black $15.00 Available
104. Evil Side Of Money, Jeff Robertson $15.00
105. Evil Side Of Money II, Jeff Robertson $15.00
106. Evil Side Of Money III, Jeff Robertson $15.00
107. Flippin' The Game, Alethea and M. Ramzee, $15.00 Available
108. Flippin' The Game II, Alethea and M. Ramzee, $15.00 Dec. 2009
109. Cater To Her, W.S Burkett $15.00
110. Blood of My Brother I, Zoe & Yusuf Woods $15.00
111. Blood of my Brother II, Zoe & Ysuf Woods $15.00
112. Hoodfellas, Richard Jeanty $15.00 available
113. Hoodfellas II, Richard Jeanty, $15.00 03/30/2010
114. The Bedroom Bandit, Richard Jeanty $15.00 Available
115. Mr. Erotica, Richard Jeanty, $15.00, Sept 2010
116. Stick N Move II, Shawn Black $15.00 Available
117. Stick N Move III, Shawn Black $15.00 Jan, 2010
118. Miami Noire, W.S. Burkett $15.00 Available
119. Insanely In Love, Cereka Cook $15.00 Available
120. Blood of My Brother III, Zoe & Yusuf Woods September 2009

Name_____

Address_____

City_____State_____Zip Code_____

Please send the novels that I have circled above.
Shipping and Handling: Free
Total Number of Books_____
Total Amount Due_____
Buy 3 books and get 1 free. This offer is subject to change without notice.
Send institution check or money order (no cash or CODs) to:
RJ Publications
PO Box 300771
Jamaica, NY 11434
For more information please call 718-471-2926, or visit www.rjpublications.com

Please allow 2-3 weeks for delivery.